HERO(INE) ADDICT

BLYTHE H. WARREN

Other Bella Books by Blythe H. Warren

Bait and Switch
My Best Friend's Girl

About the Author

Blythe H. Warren survived fifteen years of teaching before calling it quits. Now she enjoys one of those "normal" nine-to-five type jobs she used to long for. When she's not working or writing, she enjoys running marathons and honing her love of beer. She and her partner live with their rescued menagerie—three cats and a pit bull.

BLYTHE H. WARREN

BELLA
BOOKS
2020

Bella Books, Inc.
P.O. Box 10543
Tallahassee, FL 32302

Printed in the United States of America on acid-free paper.

First Bella Books Edition 2020

Editor: Ann Roberts
Cover Designer: Joseph Krystofiak

ISBN: 978-1-64247-145-8

Acknowledgments

Almost everything about my writing changed in 2018 when my sister Heidi was diagnosed with terminal cancer. She'd been an instrumental part of every book I'd written, from planning to alpha reading (is that a thing?) to editing and telling people (with polite forcefulness) to buy my books. And then, she wasn't. She wanted me to continue—no one on earth has ever loved the written word the way Heidi did—but it felt wrong, like there was a piece missing, which, of course, there was. But because I loved these characters and their story (and also because I'm not completely convinced that Heidi won't haunt me if I quit) I struggled through. But the fear of haunting alone is not enough to write a novel. Thanks to the love and support of my sister Jennie Tyderek and my partner Sue Hawks, I finished this book almost two years after I started writing it. To say it wouldn't exist without them is an understatement. I'm also indebted to my beta readers—Diane Piña, Lynda Fitzgerald, Amy Cook and Kathy Rowe. You took what I gave you and helped me make it so much better, and I'm grateful for your insight. Thank you to Michael Maginot for sharing your love and knowledge of comic books with me. You introduced me to a lovely world, and though I still have much to learn, I'm thoroughly enjoying the education. To my dear friend Ellen Joyce, I cannot thank you enough for your amazing friendship and for saving my book with your answers to my silly questions. Likewise, thanks to Meri McLaughlin for rescuing my title. I kind of love it more now. To my brother-in-law Joe Krystofiak, thank you for creating my cover and for "getting" me (not just in the "I have a super vague idea of what the cover should look like" way). To my editor Ann Roberts, you make my books better books, and you make me a better writer. "Thank you" hardly seems adequate. Finally, to everyone at Bella Books, especially Jessica, thank you for working with me. Your support and gentle nudging were exactly the sympathetic shove I needed.

Dedication

For Heidi—You made this book impossible to write and impossible not to write.

And for Jennie and Sue—Thank you for not letting me quit and for keeping my self-doubt to a minimum.

CHAPTER ONE

Harper Maxfield glanced around the deserted lobby of Golden Eagle Insurance, Inc. and sighed. It had been twenty-five minutes since she'd seen another living soul, and the phones had been notoriously quiet since she'd returned from lunch. She assumed that, like her, most people were eagerly anticipating the impending three-day weekend. In spite of mercurial weather and a too-cold-to-be-comfortably-enjoyed lake, the opening of the beaches meant that Memorial Day was the unofficial beginning of summer in the city. As a result, most of her fellow Chicagoans had taken off early to get a head start. She, however, was stuck at the currently pointless receptionist desk until five o'clock. A quick glance at her impossibly slow watch and then the it-can't-be-right clock on her computer screen, followed by a disheartening confirmation from her hard-to-deny cell phone, told her quitting time was still a painful two hours and forty-three minutes away.

She straightened the already tidy stack of files she'd organized for Floyd the intern before lunch. He'd yet to pick them up, and she began to suspect he'd snuck out early. That, or he seriously underestimated her alphabetizing skillset. Now she wished she had been less efficient in her earlier tasks, or that someone, anyone in the office, would call upon her to assist with a project. She would even settle for data entry as a way to pass the time. Sighing as another glance at her legion of damnable timepieces told her that one sad minute had passed since she last checked, she gave up hope of surviving the next two hours and forty-two minutes as the exemplary employee she normally prided herself on being.

Surveying the vacant lobby for any signs of life and seeing none, she tentatively pulled her book from her bag and opened it to where she'd left off at lunch. She was twenty pages from finishing the biography of Amelia Earhart, and even though she knew how it ended, she found the life of the great adventurer fascinating. She wasn't supposed to read (or text or tend to any non-Golden Eagle business) while at reception, but Amelia's tragic fate called to her. And there was no one around to catch her in the act, so what was the harm?

"Harper, sweetheart." She startled at the sound of Doug's oily voice and slid a file folder on top of her contraband reading material. The last thing she needed was to give him a reason to formally discipline her—an opportunity he'd likely take entirely too much pleasure in. Even in the vast lobby, being alone with him made her feel claustrophobic. She dreaded the thought of being trapped with him behind the closed door of his office.

She turned on her Doug smile—the one that looked to most people like she was digesting a cactus and pine cone salad but usually prevented him from badgering her about her preferred expression of indifference toward him—and gave him her undivided attention. He wasn't her boss, exactly, but he didn't seem to be aware of that fact.

"What can I help you with, Mr. Lawrence?" Fake half-smile firmly in place, she waited for his latest condescending response, all the while envisioning his silk tie (the cost of which could likely cover her rent twice over) tightening around his neck.

"You can call me Doug, sweetheart. You know that."

She knew but chose not to. She broadened her grin by a fraction but offered no other acknowledgment of his habitual request.

"Listen, I'm heading out for the weekend. A little early." He winked, and her stomach turned. "The wife wants to leave for the summer home before traffic gets too heavy. I tried telling her we couldn't beat the traffic if we left yesterday, but she's the boss." He threw his hands up defensively, as if Mrs. Lawrence were about to beat him into submission. If only. "Anyway, if anyone comes looking for me, just let them know I'm in a meeting with an important client and can't be disturbed."

"Of course, Mr. Lawrence. Enjoy your weekend." And now she was his involuntary coconspirator. The perks of this job were endless.

He tossed another wink her way and sauntered out the door, inspiring a wave of nausea in her.

"Come on, five o'clock," she whispered, thinking not only of a reprieve from this place, but also of much-needed time with Caroline. They hadn't seen each other all week, and she intended to do some serious catching up over the next three days, starting that night promptly at six. Harper's work friend Lainie had invited them to join her, her partner and some friends at dinner, and even though she'd never met Alice or the other women who would be dining with them, she hoped that Lainie's friends would be just as fun as she was.

Just then she heard the muffled tones of Neil Diamond alerting her to an incoming text from her girlfriend, Caroline. She smiled at the idea that they were thinking about each other at the same time, and having already violated company policy once and gotten away with it, she unearthed her phone from the clutter of her bag. Her smile faded as soon as she read the text.

Got an emergency here. Have to cancel dinner. Sorry we'll disappoint your friend. See you when I'm done.

She blinked at her phone several times, letting the plot twist sink in fully before she formulated an answer. She knew this was a possibility—it always was with Caroline. This wasn't the first time her work as a pediatric oncologist had canceled their plans for them, but since a work emergency for her likely meant that a child's life was in danger, Harper couldn't be angry. She loved how committed Caroline was to saving kids' lives. Harper should be proud of her work, not upset that it interfered with her plans.

Yet that's exactly how Harper felt—upset and disappointed. Instead of a fun dinner with her girlfriend and prospective new friends, she had the choice of sitting around waiting for Caroline, who very well could be in a justifiably foul mood, or going out alone. She read the text again, hoping for inspiration, and found herself growing irritated, not by Caroline's sudden modification of the plans they'd had for weeks, but by her presumption that Harper would just drop everything to wait for her. But why should she miss out on what could be an enjoyable evening? She'd be of zero assistance to Caroline or her patient, and though it would be rude to change the lineup so close to dinner, it would be even more inconsiderate to back out entirely.

Mind made up, she fired off a quick reply: *Unless I'm still at dinner.* Then without waiting for a response, she tucked her phone away to concentrate on the complete lack of people who needed her.

By quarter to five, most of the office had cleared out. It was just Harper, the old guard partners who would rather die at their desks than leave one second before five p.m., and a handful of others who either had legitimate work to complete before disappearing for three days or were terrified of seeming less than completely dedicated to the company.

And then there was Lainie. Harper suspected she fell into the second category of stragglers. Lainie was neither a slave to the old-fashioned notions of office propriety nor a shrinking wallflower afraid of losing her job. She ran the marketing division efficiently and expertly, and anyone who questioned her methods needed only to look at the crop of fresh clients her efforts garnered to understand that she got results, even without terrorizing the junior members of her staff. Quite the opposite, everyone in her department (and most of the office, really) adored her. Harper wished she had some legitimate reason to transfer to marketing, as working for Lainie would be amazing, even without the added benefit of escaping Doug. But even under the most liberal interpretation, Harper's degree in non-profit management couldn't be construed as being in any way related to PR or marketing.

As usual, Lainie paused at the reception desk. "We're still on for tonight, right?" Generally, she offered a sincere farewell before heading home to her partner of over two decades, but tonight, since Harper was joining them and a few of their friends for dinner, Lainie checked in. It was such a Lainie thing to do. She had a powerful position with the company, yet she always had time to make sure those with less seniority were doing well.

"Slight change in plans." She cringed before filling her in on her recent solo status.

"Not to worry, Harper. I'm sure Alice will take care of it. If she doesn't want an odd number of people for dinner, she'll find someone to fill in." Though Harper doubted how easily Alice could wrangle someone into a last-minute dinner, Lainie's genuine smile put her at ease. "Don't stick around here too much longer. It's a holiday weekend, after all."

She offered a hearty wave and headed for the elevators, leaving Harper alone with the frightened newbies and the curmudgeonly patriarchs of the firm. But with only a few minutes left to her workweek, she felt almost buoyant. The end was definitely near, and she wouldn't have to think about this place for three whole days.

"When's the last time you got out of this room?" Eliot studied her sister, whose unsettling resemblance to an extra from *The Walking Dead* couldn't be healthy.

"I'm not abandoning my daughter." Georgie's eyes were as wild as the hair that had escaped from her ponytail over the last several hours, and though she kept her voice low, there was no mistaking her intensity.

"No, but you are going to take a walk to get something to eat or at least a cup of coffee," Eliot said. Georgie didn't budge.

"You know, if you starve to death or fall over from exhaustion, Mom will blame me. Please, for my sake, give yourself a break. No one will think any less of you if you leave this hospital room for fifteen minutes."

The set of her jaw relaxed slightly. "You'll stay with her?"

"Every second. And if the doctor comes in, I'll call you immediately and trap her in the room until you get back." She stared into her sister's glassy, red eyes, her heart breaking for their collective helplessness. "I won't let anything happen to her."

Georgie stood motionless a minute longer, then grabbed her purse and phone, kissed her sleeping daughter's forehead and reluctantly stepped into the hallway.

Eliot's shoulders dropped as soon as the door closed. "It's just you and me, kid," she whispered and settled in the chair at the foot of her niece's bed where she could watch her.

The view through the window to her left was pure spring gloom and menace, the brewing thunderstorm a perfect complement to her mood, and though the overcast sky allowed little natural light into the room, with the assistance of the light pouring through the open bathroom door, it was enough for Eliot. She could see Audrey, and underneath the obvious signs of illness and the medical war against it, her resilience and strength.

Inspired, Eliot pulled a sketchbook from her messenger bag and began drawing the girl asleep before her. The soft shushing of graphite on paper blended with Audrey's rasping breaths and the symphony of medical equipment, surrounding Eliot in an eerie almost-quiet.

"What are you drawing, Zizi?" The tiny voice seemed immense compared to the near-silence it interrupted.

"You."

"Are you turning me into a superhero?" A small smile played at the corners of her mouth.

"Would you like me to?" Eliot asked, thinking it would hardly be a stretch to imagine her incredible niece as a hero. Audrey nodded, and her smile spread. "What kind of superpowers do you think you should have?"

She scooted higher in the bed and scrunched her face in thought as Eliot watched, ready to pounce on any of her needs. After carefully considering her options, she said, "I want to be a shapeshifter, like Husk."

Eliot nodded, pleased and surprised that she hadn't simply gone for flight or one of the more obvious choices. Though still in its early stages, her comics education was already developing nicely. "Anything else?"

"I get more?"

"You get whatever you want."

"I should be strong and a good fighter." Eliot almost pointed out that she already was but Audrey cut her off. "And I should have a dark past, something I'm atoning for."

She was torn between asking how much of a past a six-year-old could have and wondering where she got such an idea, though she knew the answer to that was most likely her.

"Where's Mom?"

"I made her give us some time alone, but she'll be back soon. I bet she didn't go far. I can call her to come back if you want."

"Are you going to stay with me?"

"For as long as you want me here." She stepped to the head of the bed and gently squeezed her niece's slender shoulder. "I'll always be here whenever you need me."

"Good. Okay." She nodded once perfunctorily. "What should my superhero name be?"

Eliot dragged her chair closer so they could brainstorm, and over the next several minutes, they discussed the comic book version of her niece as she lay in a hospital bed, her small body filled with chemo but both of their hearts full of hope.

Somewhere between proposing no fewer than fifteen possible aliases and deciding against a cape as part of her superhero disguise, Audrey lay back in her bed, eyelids drooping tiredly and the pillows and blankets engulfing her small body. A yawn escaped her, tapering off in a ragged breath.

Eliot tucked her sketchpad away as Audrey drifted off to sleep, cursing softly as the ringing of her cellphone cut through the stillness of the room. She fumbled to silence it, noting the caller with curious irritation.

Why would Alice be calling her now? She knew where she was, what she was doing and that the likelihood of Eliot being up for a chat was right up there with a Smiths reunion tour. Rather than answer and risk keeping Audrey awake with her conversation, she rested the phone on the tray table, amidst her coloring books and puzzles, the pitcher of water and the packets of cookies. She'd find out what Alice wanted later. For now, she set to tidying her niece's temporary residence while she rested up for the biggest battle of her young life.

She'd already received dozens of cards from family and friends, and these, along with the batch of well wishes from her classmates and teacher, hung on the wall surrounding the window. Every inch of that space filled, Eliot turned to an adjacent wall to display the latest crop of greetings from the outside world. As the stack of cards diminished, she wondered if they would run out of space before Audrey went home, hoping all the while that she was wasting her time and that, by this time tomorrow, she would have to undo her current efforts. As she affixed a particularly cheery card to the wall, she heard the insistent buzz of her phone again. Not wanting the rattling vibration to disturb her niece, she snatched it off the table, noting that, once again, it was Alice calling. Her determination was hardly surprising. This was, after all, the woman who took a spur-of-the-moment, five-hour road trip to buy a two-hundred-and-fifty-dollar bottle of bourbon as a gift for her father-in-law. Pair that tenacity with her top-notch impatience, and her inconveniently timed phone calls were the logical conclusion.

Regardless, she would have to wait. Eliot had promised both Georgie and Audrey that she'd stay here, keeping an eye on Audrey. No way would she drop her guard for a most likely frivolous conversation with her overly dramatic friend, especially since she would either have to leave the room (which she refused to do) or take the call and risk interrupting her niece's much-needed rest. It's not like she could whisper her side of the conversation, not if she wanted to be heard. Beyond that, Alice's volume control was practically non-existent. In a normal, everyday conversation, her voice carried across time zones. The possibility that, even on the other end of a phone call, she wouldn't be audible to the entire ward was too small to chance. Back in her pocket went the phone. She'd deal with that later.

By the time she positioned the last card—an adorably under the weather puppy urging Audrey to get well soon—she'd ignored two more calls despite the hint of worry that crept in. Behind her, the soft sound of the door opening pulled her attention from her active phone. Georgie, with the most hushed, calm swiftness possible, moved to Audrey's side. Her eyes fluttered open when Georgie bent to place a kiss on her forehead, and they both smiled serenely. Without looking away from her daughter, she asked, "Why haven't you answered your phone?"

"Because I promised not to let anything happen to Audrey, which is easier to accomplish when I'm not distracted. How did you know about that?"

"Alice called me when she couldn't reach you. She thinks you're being dramatic, by the way."

"Pot meet kettle," she muttered. "Of course she does. Not that I'm the one making a half a million phone calls in a ten-minute span. Did she happen to mention what she wants? She seems to have forgotten how voice mail works."

"You're invited to dinner tonight. Call her for the details." Georgie settled herself in the chair beside Audrey's bed and continued her hawk-like surveillance of her daughter.

"I don't need the details. I'm not going." She dismissed the thought of a trivial outing at a time like this.

"Do I need to remind you of our conversation earlier? You're not allowed to wither away in this hospital room any more than I am."

"But Mom won't care if I keel over." Georgie hit her with her patented impatiently incredulous look, the one she'd been throwing around since Eliot's initial brush with puberty awoke the more contentious side of her relationship with their mother. "Glaring at me doesn't make it any less true."

"We'll argue about that another time. Right now you have to get ready for dinner."

"I don't want to go to dinner. I want to stay here."

"Duly noted. But I think you should go. You deserve a break too. Just call her and see what her plans are, okay?"

Eliot balked, wanting nothing more than to sit vigil beside Audrey's hospital bed (as she knew Georgie planned to do), but her sister wasn't having it.

"If you don't at least call her, I'm going to tell Mom how you used to forge her signature on your less impressive report cards." She folded her arms across her chest and set her jaw, an obvious challenge.

"You wouldn't." As if she needed another bump in the rocky relationship with her mother. Georgie merely raised her eyebrow, her determination written plainly on her face. "Blackmailed by my own baby sister. I can't believe it." But it worked. She made the call.

"I need you to come to dinner," Alice answered, circumventing the wary greeting Eliot would have offered. "How fast can you get here?" Though she questioned the urgency of this request, Alice did sound desperate.

"First, how do you know I'm even free for dinner?" It wasn't the best opening argument, but it was a place to start and maybe get Alice somewhere closer to focused than frantic. It would be easier to decline her surprise invitation if her friend was in the neighborhood of calm.

"Because I know you. Let me guess, right now, you're sitting in Audrey's hospital room, watching her sleep and trying to will her into perfect health. You've probably been at that for hours, maybe all day, and have worn out your welcome, but your sister is too sweet to kick you out."

"That's where you're wrong. She's telling me I should go," she blurted triumphantly before realizing the emptiness of that particular victory.

"You should." Georgie's interjection earned a glare from Eliot.

"Your sister has always been the voice of reason."

Eliot snorted at this recent designation.

"It's unanimous. You're coming to dinner tonight."

"How is two against one unanimous?"

"Lainie agrees that you should come, so it's three against one."

"Still not unanimous."

"Close enough."

"With that kind of logic, I can see how you've risen in the ranks of the police department." Joking aside, she got the sinking feeling she wasn't getting out of this and dropped her head in resignation. "This isn't a setup, is it? Because you know—"

"That you're still inexplicably grieving the abrupt loss of she-who-will-not-be-named. I know all about it, and I promise this is just a group of friends breaking bread."

"Good, because I look like hell, and I don't have time to go home and clean up."

"I'm sure you look fine. Plus, you're an artist. You're allowed to be eccentric."

"Am I allowed to be a slob? Because after spending eight hours in a hospital, I'm not exactly fit for public consumption."

"Would you quit arguing and just let me buy you dinner? You deserve a little fun, kid. One night off will do you a world of good."

Her softened tone told Eliot everything she needed to know. Alice was concerned, and like everyone, wanted to do something to help. And even though she wasn't the one who needed to be taken care of, she understood the impulse. It was the same thing that had kept her tethered to this hospital room for the last two days.

"Fine," she sighed, resigning herself to the terrible fate of a nice dinner with friends. "I'll be there as soon as possible."

CHAPTER TWO

Thirty minutes into her fun, friendly evening with this mixed bag of women, Harper found herself rethinking her life choices. Not all of them, of course. She didn't mind having a college degree (even if she had yet to put it to good use), and she loved her volunteer work. That wouldn't go away.

But why hadn't she followed Caroline's lead and excused herself from this outing? Why had she stubbornly insisted on coming to a dinner full of strangers by herself? Not that she couldn't talk to strangers. Her entire career, plus her lengthy history of volunteering, reflected her skills in that area. But normally the strangers she spoke to sought something from her, and the reciprocity of their communication eased the exchange. Here, she had nothing to offer, or so these ladies seemed to think. Within five minutes of meeting her, half the table had written her off as an entitled Millennial with nothing to contribute, so she'd been reduced to polite smiling and stifling of yawns. At least if Caroline had come with her she'd have someone to talk to, and considering how close in age she was to the rest of the party, she might have provided an in, sort of like a bridge to span the generation gap that had stymied their conversation thus far.

But instead of having support for this extra social socializing, she was alone and irritated, thanks to the fight with Caroline that had kicked off her thus far disappointing evening. That hadn't been her intention, of course, but what had started as her innocently expressing her desire not to spend Friday night waiting around for her girlfriend to get out of work had rapidly escalated into her defending her intentions. Caroline, who devoted a startling amount of time to texting her in the throes of an emergency, had seemed hurt, offended and angry that Harper intended to honor the commitment they both had made. When Harper said as much, Caroline suggested that she was happy Caroline couldn't make it and that she seemed a little too eager to spend her time with other women.

Her stubborn refusal to see any side but her own, her insistence on fighting about it, even when, according to her own explanation for her absence, she should be working, were frustrating to say the least. But Harper had only herself to blame for her current mood. After all, she chose to engage. She could have told her that they could discuss it later, or she could have ignored the texts. Instead of doing the sensible thing, she'd jumped right in. She'd almost been late thanks to their argument (which she knew they would resume later), and now, on top of being part of the scenery, she was extra grumpy with no viable outlet.

Lainie and her partner aside, her present company didn't help matters much. After their initial attempts at conversation fizzled out, the woman across from her, Paige, had assumed the burden of communication for the entire party. Unfortunately, she had mastered the art of "I guess you had to be there" storytelling. While she found great amusement in every nugget she trotted out for their enjoyment, the rest of them were reduced to uttering polite sounds of something close to amusement and trying not to check the time or turn to the numbing effects of alcohol. Except Paige's partner, of course. Jocelyn's face emerged from behind her hair only long enough to nod and smile adoringly at her mate. Then back into hiding she went, like a socially awkward lesbian turtle. Harper couldn't even remember if she'd heard her speak.

She contemplated making an excuse or feigning an illness to secure an early departure. She doubted anyone here would miss her anyway. The only thing preventing her from doing that was the thought of feeding Caroline an "I told you so" opportunity. She'd rather endure a few boring hours than hand her the gift of winning this argument. Still, she looked longingly toward the bathroom, wondering how long she could reasonably hide there before it became a problem. With a sinking heart, she realized her only hope was that someone would eventually fill the vacant seat beside her and through the miracle of physical proximity manage to acknowledge her existence. She didn't dare hope that this mystery person would be likeable.

Shortly before the appetizers arrived (and in the midst of Paige's meandering and most likely pointless tale of Eastern European wanderlust in the Czech Republic), a stranger strode casually up to their table, and with a mere smile at their hosts, brought all conversation to a blessed halt (for which Harper planned to thank her would-be savior as soon as the opportunity arose).

"Eliot! You made it." Alice leapt from her seat and threw her arms around the newcomer, her effusive greeting cutting through the noise of the restaurant. Not to be outdone, Lainie also rose and joined in the enthusiastic welcome. She assumed they would all eventually be introduced to this apparently amazing specimen of humanity, but for now she was content to enjoy Paige's stupefied silence and to observe Eliot.

As she was trapped in two alternating hearty embraces, her features were as good as invisible to Harper. All she could really tell was that she was petite and seemingly unconcerned with the dictates of fashion. Alice and Lainie (both shorter than Harper) stood a few inches taller than their friend.

Eliot (who she hoped to officially meet before the arrival of the main course that they had yet to order) wore faded jeans that looked like they'd avoided more than one laundry day, and though they fit her extremely well, they seemed a bit more casual than appropriate for the trendy restaurant in which she currently stood, especially since they appeared to have a hole in one knee. Her thick, black hair was pulled into one of those haphazard ponytails that Harper would never even dream of trying to pull off. It seemed somehow sloppy and cool at one and the same time, and Harper ran her fingers through her own brown waves as if to make sure she would pass inspection. She could only guess what fashion treasure was hidden beneath the black motorcycle jacket. Despite the indifference suggested by the stranger's appearance, the woman didn't seem disrespectful or in any way unappreciative of the hospitality extended by her friends. It was almost as if she happened to walk past, saw her friends and decided to pop in and say hello.

When she finally escaped from the furious adoration of Alice and Lainie, the woman turned to greet the rest of the assembled party. She took a moment with each woman, offering a polite if distant hello to Paige, and blessing the rest of them with a broad, sincere smile. When her turn came, Harper felt herself blushing as blue eyes, vibrant and piercing even from behind thick black-framed glasses, focused exclusively on her. She couldn't help thinking that this was what it must feel like to meet a rock star.

"Eliot."

She held out a hand that Harper was slow and clumsy to accept, like she'd never encountered a handshake before and didn't know what to do with an extended appendage. "Harper. Maxfield." She cringed, wondering if she sounded too much like James Bond. "It's nice to meet you." She pumped Eliot's hand as if she expected to draw water from a well. When she realized what she was doing, she blushed again and quickly pulled her hand away, knocking over her water glass with her elbow in her haste to end the awkward greeting. At least she hadn't dumped her half-full glass of syrah directly in this woman's lap.

Unfazed, Eliot grabbed the upended glass before it rolled onto the floor and used her napkin to absorb the small lake spreading across the tablecloth. It did little to dam the flow of liquid seeping across the surface of the table, but Harper appreciated her quick action. Even more, she appreciated the gentle smile Eliot favored her with. Rather than adding to the scene that Harper had caused, Eliot treated it as a non-event, even though her lap had come dangerously close to bearing the sodden evidence of Harper's clumsiness. Everyone else, however, gasped and stared, intensifying the delightful shade of red she knew her face had become.

At last, she had everyone's attention.

If only the water spill had been the worst thing that happened. Unfortunately, it was merely a sign of what was to come. Eliot had barely sat down before the gathering devolved further, and she briefly wondered how hard the universe would work to prove that she should have stayed at the hospital.

"Please tell me that heavy coat was dictated by fashion and not the weather." Paige, who sat opposite her, looked crestfallen at the prospect of inclement weather, despite the fact that the weather had been unpredictably foul for the better part of the day. Paige shook her head in disappointment, and her short coiffed hair moved as one with her head. It was like a frosted helmet that reminded Eliot of her high school chemistry teacher (an unfortunate association as Mrs. Lake had lived to torment her). Even if they hadn't had an unsavory past, that association alone gave her amazing potential as a bumbling villain.

"Sorry to disappoint you, but I can't say fashion has ever dictated any of my choices." Eliot proved this statement by removing her coat, revealing the ultra-casual white tank top she'd relied on for comfort at the hospital. She couldn't tell if the subsequent wide-eyed regard from a third of the table had been inspired by her informal attire or the innumerable tattoos it failed to conceal. "It's even colder than it was this morning."

"But don't worry," Alice chimed in with some rare but welcome optimism. "It's supposed to get close to seventy tomorrow. Of course, Sunday looks questionable."

"And they're saying it might snow next week," Jocelyn, the ultimate wallflower, chimed in, looking surprised and terrified at the sound of her own voice. If she appeared in a comic book, it would likely be as scenery. Based on how seldom she peeked out from behind her curtain of long, graying brown hair, she would prefer it that way.

"I'm starting to believe that Mother Nature is bipolar," Paige said, a glimmer of amusement in her eye as she awaited the appreciative laughter her joke apparently merited.

"Excuse me? Did you just compare the weather to a serious mental illness?"

When Eliot had been introduced to Harper, she sized her up as either a victim or a comical sidekick—though she looked more fit than the average prey, her evident clumsiness could put her in either column. Now, with her fiery expression and the hard edge to her voice, Eliot was rethinking her initial assessment.

"It's just an expression, sweetheart." Paige looked equal parts perplexed and offended by Harper's question, like no one had ever challenged her before.

"So is, 'That's so gay,' but I don't see you championing that. Would you joke about cancer?"

"That's hardly the same thing."

"Why? Because you've been told all your life that cancer patients fight a noble battle while mental illness is shameful?"

"Because people die from cancer, and it's not their fault."

"Meaning someone with a mental illness *is* at fault? It's not like people are lining up for bipolar disorder." Despite the warning glance from Alice, Eliot relished the irritated look her interjection elicited from Paige.

"Or like they can't die because of it. Believe me, I know." That last sentence came out so softly she thought she might have been the only one who heard it, but Harper's apparent reserve lasted only a moment before she asserted herself again. "Not that the possibility of death should be the yardstick by which we measure seriousness."

Paige opened her mouth, but nothing came out. Perhaps she thought better of continuing to defend her insensitive position, or maybe she'd actually heard what Harper was saying. Either way, the argument seemed to be over, casting an uncomfortable pall over the table.

The awkward silence stretched out interminably, long enough for a cadre of waiters to deliver enough appetizers to satisfy a legion of starving diners and offering Eliot ample opportunity to study the young woman beside her—young being the operative word. She had to be ten years younger than her, which made her at least fifteen years younger than everyone else. Everything about her, from her bright yellow dress to her flawless makeup and stylishly tousled hair, screamed youth and vitality. Eliot didn't know how she'd ended up sitting at the grown-up table, but she wasn't sorry to have her there. She just wished they'd had a chance to talk before the skirmish that had managed to silence even Paige.

Just when she thought the soundtrack for their meal would be chewing noises, Harper spoke.

"I'm sorry for putting you on the spot, Paige. I hope I didn't embarrass you." Eliot noted that she hadn't apologized for what she'd said, merely for how it had been received, and Eliot was impressed, both by her maturity and her integrity. "It's an issue I'm passionate about."

To her credit, Paige didn't try to make her feel worse about her outburst. "I didn't mean to offend you," she said after a surprising, not-so-subtle nudge from Jocelyn.

"Do you ever express this passion outside of awkward dinner parties? Or do you limit yourself to challenging unassuming diners' world views?" Eliot probably should have kept her mouth shut, but she didn't see how she could make things worse. And the shy smile that crept onto Harper's face was proof enough that she'd done the right thing.

"When I'm not chastising friends of my friends, I volunteer with Mental Illness Allies. They're working to end the stigma around mental illness."

"You told me about that organization. Aren't you helping them with a fundraiser?" Lainie latched onto this potential path out from under the weighty awkwardness that had fallen over the group.

"I am. I pitched my idea to the director, and she liked it so much she put me in charge of planning it." She beamed proudly, her voice losing some of its edge.

"What's the event?"

"We're going to have a carnival later in the summer."

"Is that the best way to bring in money?" Paige asked, her surliness obviously still alive and well.

"You sound like our treasurer. She's sure this is going to be a disaster, but I intend to prove her wrong."

"Good luck," Paige snorted. "A carnival is an event for children, and children don't tend to have the deep pockets you should be looking for to sustain a non-profit."

"I agree. Don't look so shocked." Harper offered a small but genuine smile to her challenger. "I thought about all the usual fundraising events. Fancy dinners and silent auctions. They work, but if we're being honest, most of them are boring. People attend because it's a worthy cause that they want to support, not because they think they'll enjoy themselves. I want this event to be fun. I want people to want to return every year and bring their friends. The donations will come. Plus, my goal is to raise awareness as well as money. If our intention is to make mental illness less scary, to change the conversation about it, I think kids are a great place to start. They haven't made up their minds yet, and we can reach some of their parents through them."

"And the parents will definitely shell out money if you have the right attractions." Alice, who preferred to support the underdog, looked eager to pounce on this cause.

"If it comes together the way I envision it, this will be like the fun fairs we used to have at school. There will be games and prizes. We'll have lots of booths, maybe some rides if I can get a deal. And I'm looking for entertainment. The director just told me she wants an artist for caricatures. I guess she had a good experience with one when she was a kid, but so far I haven't had much luck in that department."

"Eliot can help you with that." Alice blithely volunteered her services, forgetting or ignoring the wealth of responsibilities Eliot already had lined up and waiting for her time. "She's a fantastic artist, and she knows other artists. She can be incredibly persuasive when she wants to be. I'm sure you can put her to good use."

Harper's eyes had lit up, but she tried to be graciously casual about the solution to her problem being dropped in her lap. "Please don't feel obligated. I know it's not your cause."

She didn't want to disappoint her, really she didn't, but how could she possibly commit to giving up so much of her non-existent free time?

"Before I say yes or no, I'd like to know more about the organization and why you're so passionate about it. I want to understand before I commit myself."

"That seems fair. Maybe we can meet for coffee and talk?"

Her large brown eyes were so full of hope and eagerness that she was almost grateful not to disappoint her immediately.

CHAPTER THREE

Harper couldn't believe that a night that had started so badly could end so well. True, she hadn't officially secured Eliot's artistic services (and aside from Alice's positive proclamations on the subject, she had no idea if they were even worth securing), but she felt strangely optimistic, as if her life had just shifted in some substantial but undefined way.

She wished she'd driven to the restaurant and not just because her Uber driver ignored her in favor of chattering away on the phone. Had she done so, she could have offered her potential recruit a ride home and used that time to sway her decision. But a two-day wait wasn't entirely a bad thing. She smiled, realizing that Eliot's decision to wait until Monday afternoon gave her more time to hone her sales pitch. She'd be ready to woo her new artist. She might even be so prepared and charming that she'd walk away from coffee not just with a volunteer for one day but with a new convert to the cause.

Her buoyant mood held the entire ride home as she considered how beneficial this potential alliance could be.

She imagined all the ways an artist—and one who was already sensitive to the issue—might be useful to the organization and their efforts. As she passed the darkened bakery on the first floor of her building and climbed the stairs to her apartment, she considered the astronomical improvements to their marketing alone. Even if Eliot wasn't a graphic designer, having readily available creative input would only improve their campaigns.

Once she stepped inside her apartment, however, she wished she'd found some reason to stay out longer. There on one side of the well-worn, hand-me-down couch sat her roommate Emilia, petting Mary Berry, her dainty tuxedo cat. On the opposite end of the couch, Caroline, looking poised to spring from her spot at any moment, stared straight ahead, as if not looking at her reluctant companion somehow nullified her presence. She had no idea why she'd shown up or what had compelled Em to let her in, nor did Harper know how long they'd been sitting in silence, but both of them looked relieved that she'd rescued them from each other's company.

"What are you doing here?" Her earlier good fortune had dulled her anger somewhat, but she still wasn't exactly happy to see Caroline.

"Not taking any hints," Emilia grumbled, her attention still on her lap where her orange tabby Avagato had joined his sister.

"I told you I'd come by as soon as I was free, remember?" Caroline pointedly ignored her detractor.

"And I told you I wouldn't be home. Remember that?"

"I didn't think you were serious."

Dumbfounded, she stared in open-mouthed silence. What was it with women dismissing her tonight? Had she inadvertently worn her "Please disregard everything I say" T-shirt? Being ignored by strangers at dinner had been irritating, but coming from Caroline it hurt.

"Why would you automatically assume that I was kidding about that?"

"It didn't seem like you to go off without me."

"What do you think I do all week when you're too busy working to see me? I don't hibernate. It's not like I wrap myself in a cocoon and slumber until you're ready to see me again. I have a life outside of you, Caroline, and I'm perfectly capable of functioning without you there to walk me through the incredibly difficult tasks of eating dinner and making small talk."

She noticed Emilia still sitting silently on the sidelines, taking in their argument, and based on her rapt expression and the faint glimmer of a smile playing at the corner of her lips, enjoying every second of it. If only she had a tub of popcorn and a grossly oversized beverage, her evening entertainment would be complete.

"Sweetheart, calm down."

"Don't call me sweetheart." She ground her teeth at the unfortunate reminder of Doug and the start of her difficulties that evening.

"What is going on with you tonight?"

Another glance at her roommate told her that they should move this argument somewhere more private. Not that she wouldn't fill Em in on the details tomorrow morning at the bakery, but in the moment, she didn't want to have an audience drinking in every word that she and her girlfriend spoke. And it would give Caroline one less reason to complain about her living arrangements later. Grabbing her hand, she dragged her into her bedroom and closed the door.

She took a deep breath to collect herself. No matter how insensitive she'd been, Caroline didn't deserve the full brunt of her ire. "Why did you come here, really?"

"Because I wanted to see my girlfriend. Why else would I come here? To get closer to your roommate? To listen to her thinly veiled contempt? Maybe I stopped by just to kick my allergies into high gear by spending extra time with her cats, who, by the way, shed aggressively. It's like shedding is their superpower and they want to see how much they can restrict my breathing. Probably at her behest. Why does she hate me?"

"Em can control her cats no more than she can the rotation of the earth, and don't change the subject. I told you I was going to dinner without you, so why would you think I would be home? You're not stupid, so you didn't honestly believe I'd be here."

"Maybe I was hopeful you would be." She huffed, and her expression became a blend of anger and frustration, causing Caroline to throw her hands up apologetically. "Not because I expected you to be waiting for me, I promise. I hoped that you might have finished early or been so bored without me that you would have left." She smiled in that unassuming way that got her out of trouble all the time.

"You aren't far off on that." She shook her head thinking of the mostly disastrous night she'd spent before Eliot rescued her from boredom. "It wasn't the most fun I've ever had."

"I'm sorry I couldn't be there. Would it help to tell me about it?" Gently, she sat them both on Harper's pink quilt-covered bed.

Letting go of more of her anger, Harper filled her in on the events of her evening, ending with her possible acquisition of an artist, one of the pieces of her fundraiser that she'd been stressing over for weeks, though she edited the details of Eliot's cool, attractive charm, not wanting to start another fight so soon after finishing this one.

"So, not only did your friends find a replacement for me, but it just happened to be exactly what you need?" She moved her hand to the spot just above Harper's knee where the hem of her dress fell, her fingers moving in delicate circles on the sensitive skin there. Harper nodded but said nothing, her focus zeroing in on Caroline and what she was doing with her hands. "Then what you're saying is that, by missing dinner tonight, I helped you out."

"I suppose you did, but you're still in trouble for abandoning me."

"You can punish me any way you want."

"I'm so sorry, kid. I wasn't thinking. Blame the mojitos."

Her ride had gotten barely a mile from the restaurant before Alice called, and though she was reluctant to answer (if for no other reason than her belief that human beings in her presence deserved more attention than her cell phone), she'd already ignored too many of Alice's calls that day.

"Why are you apologizing? If it's for exposing me to Paige again, then I'm afraid I can't allow the rum to be a scapegoat."

"Since when don't you like Paige?"

"Since I met her at another of your dinners and she made it her mission to defend all eight of the carnivores present from the lone vegetarian in their midst."

"I'd forgotten about that."

"That's because she didn't glare at you while telling the story of feasting on kangaroo flesh shortly after petting one."

"How did I miss that? Why didn't you say something sooner?"

"At the time, I opted not to engage out of respect for you, and since I've successfully avoided any subsequent Paige encounters until today, it wasn't worth troubling you. Had I known I could argue with her publicly and come out of it not only with our friendship still intact but also score free labor for an important cause, I might not have been so diplomatic." She kept her tone light. Though she didn't appreciate Alice's liberal sacrifice of her time, she hadn't maliciously added more stress to her life.

"If you can forgive me for appropriating your free time, I can guarantee a moratorium on Eliot-Paige reunions."

"You have a deal."

"But you have to admit, it's not the worst thing I could have done. If I had to go signing you up for community service, at least it's for someone attractive. The journey to hypertension might be worth it if that's the view along the way."

"I thought this wasn't a setup," she grumbled.

"It wasn't. I promise. But if the universe drops a semi-ideal mate in your lap, who am I to ignore the opportunity?"

"You'll be my former best friend if you don't."

"Spoilsport."

"It doesn't matter if she's attractive. I'm just meeting her for coffee so I can hear her pitch, and most likely, brush her off delicately."

"Don't dismiss this outright. After hearing her talk for just a little while, I'm interested in her organization." This was hardly a surprise. Alice collected philanthropic causes like Eliot collected comic books and memorabilia. "You might walk away from your coffee date inspired to take action. Or with a new love interest. I'd settle for either, kid."

"I'm not dismissing it outright. I just don't think I'll have the time to devote to this. And it's not a date. If it was a date, I'd take her out for something nicer than coffee."

"So you are interested."

"I'm interested in getting some sleep while I still have time to myself. Goodnight."

The end of that conversation coincided with her arrival at home, and though she wanted to call to check on Audrey, a quick glance at her watch told her she risked waking her sister and depriving her of much-needed sleep. She'd have to wait for an update, which meant she'd spend the better part of the night wondering and worrying. While she knew, logically, that Georgie would have called her if Audrey's condition had worsened or if there had been news from the doctors, that knowledge did nothing to quiet her mind.

Her unease increased when she opened her apartment door to see Scott Summers, her rescue cat, waiting for her. His one-eyed stare pierced her soul, and she calculated just how long he'd been alone. Since she regularly worked from home, he was accustomed to having her there, readily available (and ignorable). Aside from occasional shifts tending bar or her time at comic conventions, she seldom left home for such long stretches.

He narrowed his blue eye before turning his back on her and stomping impatiently in the direction of his food bowl. She doubted it was empty, but in Scott's worldview, anything less than eighty percent full was tantamount to abuse. She followed him to find not only a mostly full food dish but also that her disgruntled cat had taken out his frustrations on her possessions, providing her with ample distraction from her worry.

Somehow, he'd managed to open her cabinets and empty half a box of penne noodles on the floor (a feat her mother would surely praise him for as store-bought noodles were a cardinal sin in Carla DeSanto's world). Not satisfied with that level of destruction, he'd tipped over a bag of flour, leaving paw prints in a path from the kitchen to each adjoining room. He'd chewed and clawed at the door of the cupboard that held his food, but his biggest accomplishment there had been a smattering of tooth and claw impressions that would surely imperil her security deposit. Miraculously, he'd left her dishes alone—despite his new talent for opening doors—but her cactus, the only plant to survive her meager gardening skills, had not benefitted from the same consideration. It lay on one side of the room, its pot on the other end of a sad trail of dirt. The absence of blood assured her that he'd avoided grievous injury on his path to destruction, but the way he glared at her suggested she'd be lucky to experience the same fate.

Her exhaustion notwithstanding, instead of going to bed after dealing with Scott's mess and the root cause of his misbehavior, she parked herself at her drafting table (thankfully untouched by her temperamental cat's wrath) and put herself to work. She'd fallen behind in her rigorous schedule since Audrey's hospitalization—understandably so. But unless she got caught up, she'd undo the years she'd spent establishing herself as a reliable, sought-after artist. Then her supplemental bartending gig would become her main source of income, and tonight's dinner would be the last satisfying meal she'd enjoy for weeks. Unless she visited her mother more regularly in order to eat well, but she'd rather work all night.

Armed with a cup of black coffee, she set to work on her current favorite project. If she was going to torture herself with sleep deprivation, it might as well be at least partially enjoyable. And *The Scarlet Punisher* definitely fit that description. A smart, darkly funny, unapologetically feminist response to Straight Man Syndrome, the series was steadily growing in popularity, and her work on it was one of the proudest achievements of her career. The creator, Sara Trejo, insisted on collaborating only with women, a move that had initially led to challenges from almost every direction but had ultimately earned her respect and an appreciative, ever-expanding audience.

Over the course of a dozen books, she and Sara had established an easy collaborative relationship that sometimes extended into the bedroom when time and geography allowed.

Though she knew Sara would understand a minor delay, she couldn't ask her to live without her income any more than she was willing to go without her own. She also didn't want to risk her place on Sara's team. Not only did she enjoy the work and her relationship with Sara, but she also couldn't fathom recovering from the devastation of being dumped from an up-and-coming comic, no matter how compelling her reasons.

Determined to do her best work and finish on time, she sipped some coffee, grabbed an HB pencil and got to work.

CHAPTER FOUR

Harper rinsed the last baking sheet and dropped it in the sanitizer sink before she refilled her coffee cup for the third time. It was six thirty in the morning, and she'd spent the last forty-five minutes cleaning up after the whirlwind of Emilia in a commercial kitchen. On Saturday mornings, it took Em no time to undo all of Harper's work (a blessing for the bakery's bottom line but the wellspring of her dishpan hands and trashed cuticles). Normally she didn't mind being the Sisyphus of dishes. It was all part of the glamorous world of part-time work in her best friend's bakery. But she'd stayed up far too late with Caroline the previous night, and now even a vat of caffeine offered only minimal hope for surviving her shift. Over the rejuvenating aroma of her coffee, she detected the heavenly scents of Em at work: rich chocolate, enticing cinnamon and buttery, sugary, yeasty goodness battled for dominance. She allowed herself one more savory breath before lamenting the dishes soon headed her way.

Emilia, having been awake since three and at work not long after that, showed no signs of the exhaustion Harper felt certain should be plaguing her. Her own cup of coffee abandoned and cold, she demonstrated an impressive mastery of multitasking as she measured ingredients, mixed batter, and monitored rising dough, all while keeping an eye on the front door and the flow of customers eager for fresh pastries and the best cup of coffee in the neighborhood.

Harper noted Em's fluid movements and grace as she danced from one task to the next without hesitation. Harper preferred doing the grunt work—washing dishes, answering phones, ringing up customers—because whenever she assisted with the food prep, she felt like a ballerina in clown shoes, all awkward movements and uncertainty, but Emilia made everything in the kitchen seem effortless. It was mesmerizing, and sometimes she ended up observing her friend rather than helping her, as her role as bakery employee implied she was there to do. As she spun to remove a tray of cookies from the oven, a lock of her blond hair escaped from the red bandana that normally held it in place. It was beautiful.

"How are you still single? You should have a girlfriend." Harper hadn't meant to vocalize her thoughts and instantly regretted opening her mouth, but Em's laugh and half smirk put her at ease.

"Are you offering to fill that role? Because Caroline might object."

She ignored her not-so-subtle romantic overture. No matter how much she loved Emilia, she wasn't attracted to her. But she wasn't willing to let the subject drop entirely. "Maybe I can help."

She stopped dead in her tracks, and the large baking sheet she had been transferring to a cooling rack almost slipped from her hand. Her jaw dropped and remained slack for a moment before she spoke. "What?"

"I met someone last night who would be perfect for you." Images of Emilia and Eliot filled her head. They would make an adorable couple, and maybe going on a few dates would distract her from her second job as Caroline critic. If nothing else, it would get her out of the apartment, minimizing her exposure to the woman they couldn't seem to agree about.

"Please don't play matchmaker again. I love you, Harp, but you stink at romance."

"As the only one of us who has dated in the past six months, I'm pretty sure I'm not the one who stinks at romance. No judgment, but maybe you could use a little help, and if I happen to be in a position to provide that assistance, is there any reason I shouldn't?"

"There are about half a dozen reasons you shouldn't, starting with Cindy Mitchell." She took a tray of perfectly gooey chocolate chip cookies from the cooling rack and began arranging them on a platter for display.

"How was I supposed to know she was boring and self-absorbed?"

Up until Emilia returned angry and frustrated from her only date with the first of her attempts at matchmaking, she had thought Cindy an excellent candidate for her friend's affections. Just because she'd misjudged that situation didn't mean she'd stopped trying, as the string of bad dates with unsuitable mates attested to.

"One conversation with her would have cleared up that mystery. I appreciate your concern, but I'm really not interested in wasting time with another one of your romance orphans."

"I know I've introduced you to some duds in the past, but trust me on this. Eliot will redeem my standing as your passion proxy." She smiled broadly, her thoughts back on the perfection of this pairing.

"Don't ever use that phrase again. I'm begging you."

"Fine. My branding might not be perfect, but you and Eliot will be." Em glared at her, her patience obviously waning. "Listen, I know you'd like her. She's funny and nice, and she thinks about others and is completely gorgeous—don't tell Caroline I said that." Okay, so she didn't know if Eliot was single, but she could easily find out.

"She sounds great, but please just let me make my own mistakes, okay?"

"When are you going to do that if you never leave the house?" She eyed her friend sympathetically. "You might as well let me help you out. I think you should meet. I'm going to text her."

She slammed the empty tray on the stainless-steel countertop, the clamor reverberating through the room. "Just stop already."

"Someone's grumpy this morning."

"Someone's roommate kept her awake all night arguing with her girlfriend and then having noisy sex on the other side of a thin wall."

"We weren't that loud." Em raised an eyebrow but said nothing. "What can I say? Make-up sex is the best kind."

"That's because it's the only kind you ever have."

"Hey! Not true." She quickly looked away from another of Em's critical looks. "At least I'm having sex."

"Yeah, with someone who runs out the door as soon as she's gotten off." It was Harper's turn to glare, and Em found a batch of dough suddenly fascinating. She didn't look up from it, and her voice was gentler when she asked, "She left early again, didn't she?"

"Around two." That got a look from her, and not just any look. The "I can't believe you put up with this crap" look that she reserved for Caroline-specific situations, and a look she opted to disregard. "Did she wake you? I told her to be quiet."

"I would have had to be asleep in order for her to wake me up," she muttered and punctuated her statement with a lengthy yawn. "I didn't hear her. But if I had I might have asked what was so compelling at home that could lure her away from her girlfriend's bed. Has she ever spent the night with you?"

"Don't be like that, Em. She has a challenging schedule, and she can't just drop everything to cuddle with me." She hated that she had to explain this. Again.

"But why is that okay with you? Don't you want to spend the night with her? Don't you want someone who prioritizes you over her schedule? That's what I want."

"I don't really think I should expect to be a priority over children with cancer, do you?"

"I guess not, but do you honestly think that's what was calling her away in the middle of the night? Which of her patients paged her at that hour to come tend to them?"

She shook her head and started wiping down the front counter. She wasn't going to have this discussion again. She knew Emilia's intentions were good, but they were never going to agree on this. She loved Caroline. She didn't care that her job called her away or that her schedule was less than ideal. That wasn't what mattered. What mattered was the time they got to spend together, and that would be a lot more pleasant if her roommate wasn't around to judge every second of it. But that wasn't likely to change anytime soon.

Unless she could orchestrate a meeting with Em and Eliot. She would be mad, no doubt, but once she met Eliot, she would change her mind about going out with her. How could she not? And a moment of anger would be worth the judgment-free time with Caroline.

"I'm sorry." A plate with a slice of her favorite pie, still warm from the oven, appeared in front of her. "I get so protective of you that I forget I might be hurting you. Forgive me?"

She pulled her into a tight hug. "You know what would really earn your forgiveness, even more than pie?"

"Forget it, Maxfield," she grumbled as she headed back to the kitchen. "I'm not going on another one of your blind dates. Just eat your pie and drop it."

"Whatever you say, boss," she called after her, not deterred from her matchmaking duties in the least.

Reluctantly waking from a deep, if all-too-brief slumber, Eliot slightly opened one eye and staring back at her was Scott. He perched on her chest, and his whiskers grazed her skin as he yawned and stretched. He then pawed at her nose (without his claws, thankfully) before meowing in her face.

"You have fish breath." She reached to pet him, but he ducked her hand and meowed again. "It can't possibly be breakfast time, Scott. I haven't been asleep long enough." But a glance at her Deadpool alarm clock told her that she had managed to sleep a full hour beyond his normal feeding time. More surprising, he'd waited this long to alert her to that fact and had gone about waking her gently. His typical approach had all the subtlety of professional wrestling.

He meowed again, an elongated, plaintive yowl that clearly expressed the dire state of his starvation. Fearful that he'd resort to motivation through shredding her flesh, she forced herself out of bed and into the kitchen. Scott became a tripping hazard, keeping pace with her and winding himself around her feet, maintaining a steady chorus as they walked.

"Tripping me will be counterproductive, just so you know." He spoke again and continued with his moving obstacle course. Clearly hunger overrode logic. Or he'd decided to feast on her corpse after breaking her neck.

As soon as they entered the kitchen, he ran to his food bowl, which could only be considered empty when viewed through the eyes of a cat. He blinked at her once and then, his patience obviously at its limits, pawed at the offending bowl, scooting it in her direction. She poured out a mound of food for him, then started her coffeemaker and parked herself at the breakfast bar, hoping to stay awake long enough to enjoy the first of several necessary jolts of caffeine.

She'd finally made her way to bed less than three hours earlier. She'd completed her work for Sara's book in record time, but rather than caving to the exhaustion she'd felt earlier in the evening, she barely paused in her creative output. Unfortunately for her bank account, she didn't put that second wind to use on the other paying projects piling up at her creative doorstep. Instead, she'd turned her attentions to the character she and Audrey had started working on at the hospital.

At the time, she'd thought it nothing more than a fun distraction from cancer. Audrey had seemed to enjoy the creative process, and she had benefitted as well. She'd gone several minutes without worrying about her niece's mortality, and had instead simply enjoyed their time together.

But after devoting herself to someone else's creation, she began to see the potential in what she and Audrey had stumbled upon. Nothing in the comics world was guaranteed, of course, but she felt confident that there was something to this character and the stories they could tell through her. And if she allowed herself to be completely, terrifyingly honest, nothing with Audrey's treatment was guaranteed either. While the doctors had couched their frightening diagnosis with a slender thread of hope, they could no more ensure a full recovery than a meteorologist could promise a mild, snowless February.

So, in addition to being a fun, exciting creation, Superhero Audrey (better name pending) became a way to keep her niece with her, no matter what happened with her treatment. The more she'd considered the possibility that Audrey might not make it, the more driven Eliot had been to develop their creation. Hence the late-night artistic frenzy (yielding two dozen pages of sketches of her niece in various costumes and battle poses) and the all-consuming exhaustion this morning.

Though she would have preferred to sleep longer, her early wake up via feline presented the much-needed opportunity to tend to her overflowing hamper. Her situation was so desperate she'd had to choose between buying new underwear or going commando. Only the looming specter of her mother's disapproval made up her mind. While she couldn't be sure she and her mother would cross paths at the hospital, she had no doubt that if her mother did show up, she'd know with one glance that her eldest had opted to go panty-free that day.

And even though the value pack of plain but functional underpants she'd picked up meant that her undergarment situation was under control for the next four days, she was experiencing shortages in other areas. Mindful of her limited time, she loaded a laundry basket with as much as it would hold, and grabbing her laundry supplies, a stash of quarters and her phone, headed to the miraculously empty laundry room. Only when she headed back upstairs to squeeze in some work while she waited for the wash cycle to end did she realize that she was locked out.

Standing in front of her apartment door, she remembered that she had left her keys on the coffee table, where she dropped them last night when she got home. Most days she liked that the locks on her doors stayed locked unless a key was turning in them—one feature that sold her on the apartment (beyond its location and industrial charm) was its security. As a young woman living alone with only the protection offered by her semi-aloof and randomly disgruntled cat, she didn't want to take any chances with her safety. Now, however, she wished she'd chosen a place that was less fortressy. She so didn't have time for this. Though she knew it was hopeless, she tried turning the knob, to no effect.

"Shit." She dropped her empty laundry basket on the hallway floor and resisted the urge to kick her door. The only thing that would accomplish would be scaring Scott, and she was already on his list for her recent absenteeism. She didn't want to upset him more. "At least I remembered my phone." She praised the social indoctrination that had ingrained the habit of bringing one's cell phone everywhere. "Who I should call is the bigger issue."

Lamenting the fact that she'd lived there for over a year and had yet to establish any connection to her neighbors beyond a friendly nod or wave as they passed in the hallway, she scrolled through her contacts, considering who had spare keys to her home and who she could bother. The list of people she trusted to have access to her home was so short it almost didn't exist. Her sister and her ex-girlfriend occupied the sole positions on that brief list, which should have been trimmed by one person. She'd asked her ex to return the key, and Dina had agreed to bring it back to her. Somehow, though, their schedules never worked out, and now she was faced with the choice of bothering her sister, contacting her ex, or rappelling from the roof of her building and hoping Scott would open the window for her.

The strong possibility that Dina either wouldn't answer or be willing to help both comforted and appalled her, but she had to try to resolve this without troubling Georgie. Gritting her teeth, she fired off a text, already dreading the outcome, no matter what it might be.

Since she had nothing but time and her phone, she decided to scroll through her messages while she waited, finding one from Harper sent earlier that morning. She wasn't sure how she'd missed it, but she read it now.

It was great meeting you last night. I'm looking forward to coffee. We have so much to discuss! Just tell me where and when is best for you.

When she caught herself grinning, she immediately dismissed her reaction as the result of fatigue and retreated from the correspondence. She'd answer Harper later, when she wasn't so muddleheaded and could trust herself to be professional. Clearly sleep deprivation freed her of a sound mind.

Fifteen minutes later, when her ex still hadn't responded, she acknowledged the likelihood that she was still asleep. Probably in the bed of some nubile, imbecilic arm candy like the apparently irresistible jailbait who'd brought their relationship to an end. If she rolled out of bed by noon, it would be a supernatural occurrence and entirely too late to do her any good. Resigning herself to making Georgie's life even more complicated, she reached out to her sister and hoped for the best.

Georgie answered after the first ring. "Audrey woke up long enough to ask if she could add time travel to her skillset. I assume this is your handiwork."

"I may have had some influence." She smiled at the thought that Audrey was as obsessed with their creation as she was.

"Are you on your way?"

"Not exactly," she admitted and explained her predicament. "I'm waiting to see if Dina can come let me in. She should still have a spare key unless she threw it away."

"Why would you invite her back into your life? And why does she still have a key?"

"I know I've made no secret of my love of Spider-Man, but that doesn't endow me with the ability to scale walls. Nor can I pass through solid material like Kitty Pryde, so unless you'd like me to take up residence in my hallway, I have no other options."

"I can be there in twenty minutes," she said, like it was the most obvious solution in the world.

"You're just going to leave Audrey by herself?"

"Vinnie is here. He just got back this morning and came straight to the hospital. I think maybe Audrey and her father deserve some time together, and since my big sister has gotten herself into trouble and needs my help again, I probably should take care of her. Or I could give Mom your keys and send her over if you'd prefer."

"I'll see you in twenty minutes," she said before making herself comfortable.

CHAPTER FIVE

By the time Georgie appeared at the far end of Eliot's hallway (closer to thirty minutes than the twenty she'd promised), Eliot had transferred her laundry from the washer to the dryer, sent Dina a follow-up, ignore-my-last-message text and had worked herself into an anxious mess. Her sister, by comparison, seemed calm as she strolled down the hall, an impression amplified by her painfully moderate pace. If not for the fact that she was there to rescue her from her own absentmindedness, she would have snapped.

Her lack of urgency continued once they were inside her apartment. Rather than turning around immediately after unlocking the door or trying to rush Eliot, she poured herself a glass of water and sank onto the couch beside Scott, who was deeply involved in vital grooming of his belly. Eliot, who was about to embark on the fastest shower in the history of indoor plumbing, paused in her frantic preparations to eye her sister quizzically.

"Don't you want to get back to the hospital?"

"I can wait for you to get cleaned up. You look like hell. No offense."

"I can just meet you there. I have to wait for my clothes to dry anyway. Unless I want one of my more thoughtful neighbors to dump half my wardrobe on the laundry room floor."

"I don't mind waiting." She sipped her water and looked everywhere but at Eliot.

"What's wrong?" She sat beside her, forcing Scott to grumble and jump off the couch. "You're acting weird."

"I'm acting fine. I came to help you, which I did, and now I'm waiting for you because it doesn't really make any sense for me to come over here just to return empty-handed. Audrey's expecting her Zizi."

"Last night I had to force you to leave her for fifteen minutes, and now you're happy to waste time petting my cat."

"I don't think Scott agrees it's a waste of time."

"Why are you avoiding the hospital? What happened?"

"I told you, I think Vinnie needs some time with his daughter."

"Weren't Mom and Jimmy there?"

"Not everyone gets thwarted by locks."

"Then the quality of that quality time is going to be seriously limited."

"But I also need time with my sister." Tears welled in her eyes, and before they could fall, Eliot had pulled her in for a tight hug.

"What's wrong?"

"I'm pregnant."

She leaned back to look in her sister's eyes. "You're more upset now than when you got knocked up in college. At least you don't have finals to study for. Why aren't you happier?"

"It's just the worst timing ever. Audrey's sick. I have to take care of her. I can't do this. I can't be pregnant now."

"I'm no expert, but I think you've already proven otherwise. And what's there to do? It's not like you have to manually divide the cells. Just carry on as usual and let biology do the rest."

"What if it doesn't work?"

"Which *it* are you referring to?"

"Audrey's treatment. What if it doesn't work, and she...and then I have this new baby, and it's like I'm replacing her."

"Oh, sweetie. It's not like that at all, and no one who knows you would ever think that."

"*I* thought it."

"You're scared and letting your fears take over. You aren't replacing Audrey. It would be impossible. Just enjoy this moment. It's a good thing."

"What if," she faltered again, and Eliot squeezed her hand gently. "What if this baby gets sick too?"

And there it was, what her sister was really worried about. "Then we'll get through it together."

"I don't think I can do this again."

"I think you're underestimating what you're capable of, but who says you'll have to? What are the chances that this baby will have the same issue? Look at us. We don't even have the same eye color."

"I think it's more complicated than that."

"So let's talk to someone who can give us answers, maybe part of that team of doctors taking care of Audrey could answer your questions. In the meantime, let yourself be happy. This is a big deal, you know? Another child gets the gift of me as an aunt. You're doing the world a favor."

"You're an ass. And a really good big sister."

"I can give Audrey some tips."

"Thank you." They hugged again before Georgie pushed her gently away and wiped her tears. "You really need a shower."

"I'm not the one who interrupted that mission with her big news."

"I have something else to talk to you about."

"If you tell me Mom is pregnant too, I'm going to have to throw myself out the window."

"At this point, I think Mom's as likely to get pregnant as you are." She picked up a nearby sketchbook and began flipping through it, not really stopping on any page long enough to appreciate the work, but Eliot took advantage of her distraction and got in the shower, leaving the bathroom door open for easier communication.

"What are you saying about Jimmy?"

"Can you not talk about my dad and sex ever again, please?"

"Gladly. What did you want to talk about?"

"Audrey's birthday is next weekend."

"I haven't forgotten."

"We weren't going to have a party because she might still be in the hospital, but then we realized that this, um, this might be our last chance to celebrate."

"It won't be," she said, not at all sure she was right.

"Anyway, we're having a birthday party, location TBD, and we'll need a cake. I was sort of hoping you could bring one."

She popped her head around the shower curtain, shampoo suds dripping on the floor. "I didn't realize this was a suicide mission."

"Don't be dramatic."

"I don't have time or the skill to bake anything our mother will find acceptable, and you know what will happen if I show up with a store-bought cake. You don't trust her ability to find things to criticize on her own? You have to supply her with material?" She scowled at her sister's pained eye roll. "Why can't she make the cake? We'll all be happier."

"She's already making dinner, and she's not getting any younger. I thought it would be nice to give her a break."

"By sacrificing me?"

"It won't be that bad. I already told her I was asking you."

"And how did she take that?"

"Not nearly as catastrophically as you'd like to believe."

"Twenty dollars says she shows up with her own cake, just in case I happen to live down to her expectations."

"I'll take that bet if it means you'll do it."

"Fine. I'll supply the cake. Any other ways I can throw myself on the sword, or rather the cake knife for you?"

"Not at the moment, but I'll let you know if that changes."

Her exhaustion notwithstanding, Harper's morning had been a good one. True, there was the brief spat with Emilia, which was due as much to their shared sleep deprivation as to their long-standing habit of semi-regular sparring over mostly minor things. And like most of their mini-arguments, it had blown over quickly with no real damage done—and she got free pie out of it. Nothing that ended in free pie could be that bad.

And though she hadn't heard back from Eliot yet (even though she'd sent a text shortly before she clocked in at the bakery, which translated to ungodly early for most of the world), she couldn't help feeling optimistic. On top of getting the help she needed for her fundraiser, she might have stumbled upon true love for her best friend—that was, if Eliot ever replied. She'd also gotten her weekly dose of Mr. Sutcliffe's good mood and generosity, something she looked forward to every Saturday morning. He was by far her favorite regular customer, and she admired the fact that he didn't let any of the misfortunes he'd endured in his eighty-plus years weigh him down—watching his wife of fifty years succumb to the heartbreaking ravages of Alzheimer's and losing his son in a fire. She could learn a lot from his example, and every time he repositioned his tweed cap on his balding head and offered a chipper farewell, she vowed to be more like him. A solemn oath that generally fell by the wayside by Wednesday morning.

Her mood dipped a little when, shortly before the end of her shift, Caroline sent her a text canceling their plans. Not that they'd had anything spectacular scheduled for that evening. They hadn't had much time to discuss how to spend their Saturday night together before she sailed out the door in the early hours of the morning. But the intent to spend time together had been there, and now she'd been cast aside in favor of work. She couldn't get mad—Netflix, wine, and cuddling hardly took precedence over whatever medical emergency had usurped her this time, but every once in a while (and she would never admit this to anyone), she wished she came in first. She supposed that was just the downside of falling for someone with such an important career. Caroline saved people's lives—regularly. What did her work contribute to the world? A pleasant phone voice and brief hold times? It hardly compared.

She was ready to wallow, forgetting her Mr. Sutcliffe vow an impressive four days early, when the bell above the door jingled, and she looked up to see her mother, a smile to rival her favorite octogenarian's, breezing into the shop. She instantly dropped what she was doing and ran to give her the strongest hug she could, still no match for the warmth of the embrace Mrs. Maxfield returned.

"What are you doing here? I thought we were having lunch tomorrow."

"Can't we do both?" They squeezed each other once more for good measure before they moved arm in arm to one of the tables Harper had just cleared. "I missed my baby girl, and I know that, between work and your social life, you won't have much time to talk on the phone today, so I thought I'd just pop in and say hello and maybe pick up some of those delicious cookies Emilia makes."

"I'll pack up a box of anginetti for you, Mrs. M., on the house." Emilia's sudden appearance at their table reaffirmed Harper's suspicion that her roommate was part cat.

"Nonsense, Emilia. I insist on paying."

She waved off Mrs. Maxfield's offer, and taking advantage of the brief lull, took a seat next to Harper.

"My social life isn't going to be that time-consuming today," Harper confessed, "but I'm glad the threat of my popularity brought you here. I missed you too."

"No date tonight?" The surprised question hit her from both women, like a chorus of surround-sound sympathy laced with contempt. She knew they meant no harm, but she didn't really want to talk about Caroline's most recent disappearing act.

She shook her head and considered explaining, but the story wasn't a new one. And though neither of them would ever suggest that sick kids weren't important, they also never seemed to agree that Harper shouldn't also be important. It was an endless battle, and she didn't have the energy to fight it right now.

"The night doesn't have to be a complete loss." Em perked up at the thought of whatever she was about to propose. "We could go out tonight."

"Aren't you exhausted? I can't believe you want to do anything other than fall into bed after you finish here."

"It's been ages since we've done anything fun. And my mom opens the bakery on Sundays, so I get to sleep in."

"Only you would consider a six a.m. wake-up call sleeping in."

"Come on. This is the perfect opportunity for us to have some fun."

"You two should go dancing." Breezing past her reluctance, her mother chimed in with suggestions for fun. "You always used to go dancing together. And it's a great way to meet people. For Emilia, of course."

"Your mom has a point, Harp. You should listen to her, especially since you kind of said the same thing earlier."

There really was no reason for her whole Saturday night to be a complete waste. Just because she couldn't see Caroline didn't mean she still couldn't have fun, and though she wasn't ready to give up on her vision of Em and Eliot making the perfect couple, it wouldn't be a bad thing for Em to get out and blow the dust off her dating skills.

"Okay. I'm in. Tonight, we dance."

Eliot wasn't terribly surprised when it took her mother less than two minutes to criticize her. To be fair, the stress and uncertainty they'd all been living in recently would challenge even the healthiest relationship, which meant that a peaceful encounter with her mother would border on miraculous. And if miracles existed, she'd rather reserve hers for Audrey.

"That's what you're wearing?"

"No, it's an illusion. Realistic, right?"

"This is a hospital, not a floozy convention."

"Did I get those confused again? My floozy membership is in peril after a blunder like this."

"You're about as funny as you are ladylike."

"What's so shameful about my outfit?"

"There's less to it than a Barbie dress."

"It's a tank top and jeans, not a thong bikini. And since when does the hospital have a dress code? Have you seen the gowns they hand out?"

"I just wish you'd dress more like a lady."

"I'm dressed like a lady who has to go to work tonight and didn't want to miss time with her family because she had to go home and change."

"Well, at least you still love your family."

"Always," she said, hoping to put this snarl behind them.

"But if you'd just get a regular job with a normal schedule, you wouldn't have to run off all the time. Of course, with all those tattoos—"

"Why don't we just leave it at loving your family?"

She was surprised to hear typically reserved Jimmy cut his wife off, especially since it was to her benefit. Carla bristled at the interruption, but she didn't return to whatever unflattering comment she was about to make about Eliot's appearance. She and Vinnie exchanged surprised glances as a mostly peaceful quiet fell over the room.

"How did last night go?" Georgie's voice cut through the silence, and Eliot shot a death stare her way. She hadn't meant any harm, but since she hadn't spent close to three decades keeping her guard up around their mother, she wasn't well versed in subterfuge. If it wasn't harmful to her, Georgie's innocence would almost be refreshing.

"What happened last night?" Her mother seemed innocent, but this would only get worse.

"I had dinner with friends." She doubted her evasive maneuvers would work, but it didn't hurt to try.

"Mom said you had a date." Even Audrey was betraying her. This was a nightmare.

"Your mother has a vivid imagination." She glared at her sister again, wondering how on earth she concluded that a last-minute dinner with Alice was anything close to a date, and how that next-to-nonexistent possibility became news worth spreading to her daughter.

"Why wasn't it a date?" Audrey looked like a baby bird peeping out of her nest of blankets. Eliot hated disappointing her and hated more that she'd been put in this position.

"I was wondering the same thing," her mother chimed in. "Do you need me to set you up with a nice girl? Your father works with some lovely young women at Streets and San. He could introduce you."

She didn't care if the rest of Jimmy's crew consisted of Charlize Theron, Lupita Nyong'o and Jennifer Lawrence. She was not resorting to hookups from her stepfather. "It was never supposed to be a date. In fact, that was one of the conditions of me going. It was just supposed to be dinner with friends, and it was fine. Just a bunch of middle-aged women drinking too much wine and complaining about their mundane lives." The less they knew, the better.

"We need more than that, El, and we're not above harassing you until you talk. You'd be better off just giving in now."

Her sister was right, of course, not that it made her eager to discuss the previous evening or any other details of her life. "There were appetizers and drinks. Two women got into an argument. Alice volunteered me to help with a fundraiser, and we had dessert. That just about wraps up my fun Friday night."

"You're volunteering now?" Her mother broke her short-lived silence. "How are you supposed to find time for that? We barely see you as it is."

"I'm not. Probably. I promised the young woman running the fundraiser that I'd meet with her. That's all. But I haven't even had a chance to answer her text about the meeting." A momentary twinge of guilt hit her, but she didn't dare pull out her phone during what her mother would consider family time.

"If she's a pretty young woman, I foresee a sudden upsurge in philanthropic activity."

She glared at her sister once more but kept her mouth firmly shut on the topic of Harper's looks.

CHAPTER SIX

Harper had never been to this bar before, but she felt as if she had. The bass of the music thumped its way from the dance floor and into her chest, just as it would have in any other nightclub. The same dim lighting as always afforded affectionate couples the illusion of privacy (sporadically interrupted by hectic bursts of light from the crowded dance floor), and despite having opened two short months earlier, that familiar bar smell of stale booze permeated the air. The only thing that separated this place from the rest stood behind the bar—Eliot. She mixed drinks and charmed the tips out of a horde of swooning lesbians clamoring for their chance to woo the gorgeous, tattooed bartender in the form-fitting white tank top.

She couldn't exactly blame these women for ignoring the other bartender (a weathered, bleached blonde whose charm paled in comparison to her coworker's) and waiting for their turn with Eliot. She was stunning and totally in her element. Her body—compact and oddly elegant with its wealth of ink—was hard to ignore. If not for the adorably nerdy glasses she had to keep pushing up, she would be almost unapproachably hot. But thanks to that touch of disarming humanity, she was the right blend of attractive and accessible for her friend.

Harper caught herself following her every movement as she stretched, bent, pivoted and maneuvered around her fellow bartender to fill drink orders. Suddenly she felt incredibly thirsty.

"Let's get a drink," she called out as one song bled into the next. Em didn't hesitate to follow her as she snaked her way through the crowd.

She wished she'd realized her good luck before they'd shimmied their way through three songs. Ideally, Em would look her well-groomed best for this life-changing introduction, but she wasn't about to let this opportunity pass them by.

As they waited somewhat impatiently for Eliot to clear the line of thirsty patrons in front of them, the other bartender finished with her last customer and tried calling them over to her. Em was about to head over there, but Harper insisted they stay put. "We're next anyway, and by the time we get down there, someone else could walk up to the bar in front of us."

"What's the difference if we wait there or wait here?"

She wished she could explain without revealing her ulterior motives. The last thing this introduction needed was Emilia's palpable irritation. "I just feel like this is the bartender for us. I mean, she has to be more skilled to have so many more people waiting for her to mix their drinks. And we should get the best drinks possible. Don't we deserve that? Isn't that what tonight is really about?" She was trying too hard but couldn't seem to stop herself.

"What if she's just slow, not skilled? Not that that would stop these ladies from waiting. Look at her."

"You think she's attractive?"

"Only to those with a pulse. And why are you smiling like that? Just because I can recognize that the woman is attractive doesn't mean I'm going to go for it with the bartender."

"But it doesn't mean you won't."

"You think that's my speed?"

"Just wait until you talk to her. She's not nearly as intimidating as she seems."

"I thought this was your first time here. How do you know how intimidating she is?"

"Because that's Eliot, the woman I was telling you about. The one I wanted you to meet."

"Is that why you wanted to come here? Because I'll leave right now."

"I had no idea she worked here. I promise. I thought she was an artist. It never occurred to me that she would have a side job or that it would be here. Please don't run away from this."

"Whatever you say." She frowned but made no attempt to leave.

In spite of Em's darkened mood, Harper anticipated receiving heartfelt thanks in just a few minutes, especially since her work was already half done for her. Em already found Eliot attractive, and what were the chances that Eliot could look at her—with her curly blond hair, expressive green eyes and curvy in all the right places figure—and not feel the same attraction? This setup was as close to a sure thing as any of them were likely to get.

Harper turned her attention back to Eliot and noted the easy way she flirted with her customers. That was a little troubling, but she supposed it made sense. She wanted to make good tips, and what better way to achieve that goal than charm and flattery? That didn't explain why it was taking her so long to serve the obnoxiously giggling pair of ladies who'd been hogging her attention for the last five minutes, however. Honestly, how long did it take to pour two glasses of cheap white wine? They should have been out of the way several hair flips ago, but there they stood, obstructing true love and prolonging her thirst. Something had to be done.

"Shouldn't you be conquering the art world and ignoring people's texts?"

Eliot looked up into the eyes of the last person she expected to see standing at her bar. Technically, her mother (followed closely by Jimmy) would be less likely, but it would also be considerably more awkward if her mother was smiling at her like that. And her mouth probably wouldn't have gone dry at the sight of her in painted-on jeans and a black V-neck camisole (at least not in a good way).

"Do you pick fights with virtual strangers every time you go out, or have I just managed to catch you on your best days?"

"Consider yourself lucky. Most people only get to see my chipper, friendly side. Of course, they also don't ignore me for an entire day. They're quirky like that."

"Fine, I surrender. I'm sorry for waiting so long to answer you."

"Except you didn't answer." She leaned so far across the bar that Eliot couldn't help getting a glimpse of her cleavage. To distract herself from that glorious view, she whipped out her phone and sent a quick reply.

"Better?" she asked when Harper checked her most recent message.

"Perfect," she said after glancing at her phone. Apparently she felt the need to text the same thing, possibly to prove a point.

"Did you want to order a drink or did you just stop by to harass me?"

"Both. I'm up for all kinds of fun." She grinned mischievously and turned to a blonde beside her, drawing her attention to the petite woman for the first time. "What do you want, Emilia?"

"Apparently, we'd like the same thing," she grumbled.

Harper, who'd perched herself on a recently vacated barstool, leaned enticingly forward, and, chin in hand, asked, "What do you recommend?"

"I guess we're staying here a while," the blonde muttered and moved closer.

"What are you in the mood for?"

"I'm up for anything." Harper's impish grin grew broader.

"You didn't drive, did you?" She shook her head no. "Have you eaten recently?" She shrugged a non-answer. "You're only allowed one of these, then."

Belatedly, Eliot introduced herself to the increasingly irritated blond woman (and likely girlfriend), Emilia, who tried to pay, but she stopped her.

"The first round is on me for being so inattentive earlier." She threw a wink at the pair, and as she turned to help the next customer, she bumped into her fellow bartender.

"Not bad." An appreciative grin accompanied the comment.

"Don't ogle the customers, Sheryl."

"You had no problem with that a minute ago with the tall cutie."

"At least I'm free to look. Doesn't your girlfriend take issue with you objectifying the clientele?"

"She subscribes to the Dolly Parton philosophy of commitment." She raised her eyebrows in a question. "It doesn't matter where I build up my appetite as long as I come home to eat."

"I'm sorry I asked."

She took one satisfying sip of her undeniably potent cocktail before she realized that Emilia was staring at her. "What?"

"What are you doing?"

"Enjoying my drink. Have you tried yours yet? It's really good. If she's half as good an artist as she is a bartender, my worries are over."

"What was that with Eliot?"

"What do you mean?"

"All the flirting."

"We were just talking. I wasn't flirting with her."

"Okay. Except you were." Silently, she waited for the explanation she was sure was forthcoming. "The smile, the lean, the teasing and banter? That was some of your best work. Very kittenish."

"That wasn't flirting. You're acting like I slid her my number on a napkin."

"You didn't have to. She already has it. Remember when she interrupted the playful banter to text you? I don't know what she wrote, but it got a smile out of you and a scowl out of every woman nearby who just watched her shot with the hot bartender go up in flames."

Exasperated, she showed her the far from flirty text: *Monday at one, coffee shop on Fairbanks and Erie.* The only part that could come close to being suggestive (but fell far short of the mark) was the smiley face emoji at the end.

"You're making more of this than it is. We were just having a friendly conversation. Besides, you weren't stepping up, and one of us had to be friendly."

"No, one of us didn't. It's not a requirement to flirt with the bartender, no matter how attractive she might be."

"So you do think she's attractive." She did her best to ignore her long-suffering stare. "When she comes back, you can flirt with her."

"Like hell am I following that performance."

"But how are you going to fall in love with her if you don't get to talk?"

She looked from her to Eliot before answering. "Somehow I don't think that limited conversation will be the biggest obstacle to our relationship."

CHAPTER SEVEN

Eliot checked her watch for the fourth time in five minutes, her agitation growing with each tick of the second hand. She still had ten minutes to kill before her appointment with Harper, and all she wanted to do was leave. She'd anticipated the difficulty of walking out of her niece's room to come to this fruitless encounter, but she hadn't counted on any positive developments compelling her to stay.

She'd assumed Audrey would be sleeping (she did that a lot lately), not animatedly talking with the third doctor who'd delivered a variation on the tentative good news they'd received that morning. The fever that had contributed to her hospitalization had gone down, and her labored breathing, another factor in her extended stay, had markedly improved. The doctors wanted to monitor her after chemo the following morning, but if all went well, she might be home for her birthday. And though the doctors' perfectly reasonable postponement of her release was frustrating, she tried not to let that minor disappointment override her joy about the otherwise good news.

Leaving had been a challenge and staying away was next to impossible, but she didn't want to cancel on Harper at the last minute. Not only was it rude, but she also didn't kid herself that she would get out of this meeting so easily. Considering the backlash for one ignored text, the ensuing harassment to reschedule a meeting would be out of control. And the sooner she declined, the better off they'd both be. She could put her focus back where it belonged—family and work—and Harper could continue her search for an artist. Maybe she'd even give her some leads to follow.

So, rather than waiting around for yet another doctor to deliver the same frustratingly good news, she'd forced herself out the door early. And now she sat nursing her eighth cup of black coffee that day, hoping it could get her through this meeting and the day. But she was already contemplating a refill.

To distract herself from the imperceptible passage of time, she flipped to a clean page in her sketchbook and began drawing an older woman who sat on the opposite side of the café, her worn and grimy raincoat pulled tightly around her. On any other day, she would delight in bringing the craggy wrinkles of her face and the mass of unkempt hair to life on the page. She could easily lose herself in the beauty of her rheumy eyes and the weathered face that suggested a life fully (if not always happily) lived. Today, however, she was too easily distracted by the painfully sluggish movement of time, the impending arrival of the young woman she was about to disappoint and her niece's encouraging prognosis. More than once she found herself glancing at her phone in case her watch was slow, and her meeting was closer than she thought. It wasn't.

She supposed that, if she had to be away from her family, there were worse distractions than coffee with a kind-hearted, funny and admittedly attractive young woman. Though she'd dismissed Sheryl's comments on Saturday, she'd had a hard time since denying there was some truth in them. She'd thought about Harper at least half as much as she'd thought about Audrey, which was twice as much as she should have. Not that she was planning on pursuing anything with her, since her blond companion, whose persistent and irritated presence at the bar suggested she was the girlfriend, meant that she was off limits. But that didn't mean she couldn't still enjoy her company.

Returning to her sketch of the older woman across the shop, she again tried to lose herself in drawing. She made roughly a dozen more lines before a flushed and flustered Harper burst through the door and rushed to the table, leaving her to abandon the woman on the page with only one eye and half a nose.

Harper didn't know why she was so nervous. It wasn't like she'd never done this before. True, specifically soliciting an artist was new, but she'd already secured food vendors, games and tents (with still more to come), and while most of her contacts had been kind, friendly and open-minded, not all of them had been a dream to work with. But she'd stayed calm and poised, and eventually she'd gotten what she needed from each of them, even if that was the number of someone more pleasant and accommodating to work with. With those exchanges, she hadn't had the benefit of an established familiarity. By comparison, this should be as easy as the alleged flirtation at the bar on Saturday, nothing to stress about, especially since an artist wasn't vital to her event's success. If this were the cotton candy vendor, she'd have good reason to be anxious, but no matter how fun the head of Allies thought this would be, it wouldn't be the end of her fundraiser if Eliot said no.

The fact that she was running late did little to settle her already overtaxed nerves. She wanted to blame Caroline—after all, she had delayed her by close to thirty minutes. If not for her surprise visit before work—on a holiday no less, which just proved what an amazing, caring person she was, not at all the selfish boor Emilia liked to think her—Harper would have arrived at the coffee shop early, as was her plan. She supposed she could have said no, ignored the gentle kisses on her neck and the strong hands massaging their way down her back. She could have pretended the tongue tracing her earlobe had zero effect and told her in no uncertain terms that she had an appointment and didn't have time. But she realized they wouldn't get a chance to be together again for days, and before she knew it, her blouse was on the floor, her pants were undone and she was on her back. Now she'd be running into her meeting out of breath and discombobulated, and she'd be lucky if she got to have the latte she'd been looking forward to since she woke.

As she raced to the appointed coffee shop ten minutes late (and thirty minutes after she intended to arrive), she glimpsed the sterile scenery around her, realizing that they were meeting in the heart of the hospital campus where Caroline worked. Building after building proclaimed its affiliation with the hospital, and there, nestled among the doctors' offices, labs, surgical centers and various other medical facilities, was the coffee shop, a lone retail island in a sea of healthcare. It was entirely out of the way and a minor challenge to find unless you knew what you were looking for. As such, it seemed an odd choice for this meeting.

She took a moment to collect herself before rushing through the door, sensing that an out-of-breath, slightly sweaty beggar had even less chance of being a chooser. The obvious evidence of her attempt at timeliness might earn her some forgiveness, but it probably wouldn't project the image she wanted, so after a deep breath and one more reassurance that she could do this, she threw open the café door, plastered on her brightest smile and made her way to Eliot's table.

"I'm so sorry I'm late." She opened with an apology to appease both her audience and her fear that she'd blown this meeting before it even started, but Eliot glanced at her watch and smiled.

"I run on artists' time, so you're actually early."

"But you still beat me, so I think maybe you're just being nice."

"That happens sometimes if I'm not careful." She winked, and Harper blushed, feeling embarrassed and generally out of sorts as this meeting drifted a little farther off track. "And now I'm going to be even nicer and offer to buy you a coffee."

"You bought last time, so this round is definitely on me." She tried a wink of her own, felt the awkwardness of it in her entire face and then compounded her mortification by saying, "Name your poison."

In this moment, she thought she could write the guidebook for dorkiness, and she gratefully retreated to the safety of the counter to place their order. She hoped that the most embarrassing part of this meeting was now behind her. But she doubted it.

"I know you haven't officially agreed to help yet, but thank you for at least hearing me out." She placed a perfectly foamy conciliatory cappuccino in front of Eliot and donned her winningest smile. "Fair warning. Once I start talking about Allies, getting me to stop is almost impossible, so if there's anything you want to ask, now might be the best time."

"Tell me about Allies. What do they do?"

"We work to improve the lives of people with mental illness."

"In what ways?"

"Part of it is day-to-day stuff, like navigating insurance and helping with housing and employment. But our larger focus is education, for the patients, for their families and friends and for the general public. The more people understand mental illness, the less likely they are to alienate others. Sometimes, like with Paige, people just don't think about what they're saying and how it might offend someone."

Apparently, she was even less riveting than usual. Within two minutes of launching on her favorite topic, she lost Eliot to her sketchbook. While Harper supposed this could act as the portfolio she saw no signs of, it was mildly unnerving to share intimate eye contact one moment only to lose that attention to whatever she was drawing.

"Um, there are plans for a twenty-four-hour hotline, not just for suicide, but for any issue, like feeling alone or struggling to get out of bed. I'd like to extend that to advocates as well, to help friends and family members better handle a loved one's diagnosis. But we don't have the resources for that yet."

"Hence the fundraiser." Eliot popped her head up for the span of her brief comment and then back to the page went her attention. It was a little like trying to have a serious conversation with a prairie dog.

"Exactly. But for me, the most important part of our mission is working to end the stigma of mental illness."

"How did you get involved with Allies?" She again glanced up, and the unexpected warmth of her blue eyes (even more startling in comparison to her previous view of the top of her head) unsettled Harper, making her forget for a moment the question and the time of day and possibly even her own name. Never mind devising a coherent answer.

"High school," she bleated when she could again formulate thought. Eliot's brow creased as she lifted her eyebrows in perfectly understandable confusion. She had, after all, reduced a long, complicated story to two somewhat meaningless words that instilled dread, loathing and traumatic flashbacks in most. "I heard about them when I was a freshman, but I had to wait until my junior year to work with them. Most kids look forward to getting their license when they turn sixteen. I couldn't wait to start volunteering."

She cleared her suddenly dry throat and reached for her coffee, bumping the mug and sloshing some of the contents onto the table. Thankfully, Eliot's sketchbook was safely in her lap for the great latte overflow.

"Why mental illness?" Apparently unfazed by Harper's clumsiness or the creeping pool of espresso and milk, she threw a couple paper napkins on the spill and carried on with the conversation and the drawing as if nothing unusual had happened.

"My brother." She offered another oversimplification, this time out of self-preservation, and stared out the window for a moment, reflecting on their past and hating herself for her selfishness.

She remembered the night, just a few weeks before he died, when she'd made him take her to the movies—a picture her parents didn't think she was mature enough to see. He was home from college for the weekend and obviously depressed. Whether that sprang from his illness, some difficult life event or a combination of the two, she didn't know. The last thing he wanted to do was sneak his kid sister into a movie theater potentially full of people he used to know and didn't want to see.

She should have understood that and respected his limitations. Instead, she begged him relentlessly, harassing him for hours until she finally wore him down.

He'd been closer to happy as they rode the train to the theater, but once they took their seats, his depression reasserted itself, bringing an unhealthy dose of discomfort with it. It was like he thought everyone in the theater was watching him, like they knew he was bipolar, and they were judging him or waiting for him to act crazy. She'd known how uncomfortable he was, how much he was suffering and wanted to go home or hide, but she'd ignored his distress, caring more in that moment about her own enjoyment than his well-being.

"He's bipolar?" The question brought her back to the present.

"Was." She tried to swallow the lump in her throat. This wasn't what she came here to discuss, and she wasn't prepared to relive the past, not if she wanted to remain professional and have a chance of getting Eliot's help. She didn't have the luxury of time to indulge in memories of Blake.

"Why nonprofit work? Why not psychology?"

"Blake had a psychiatrist, a very good one. What he needed was support and understanding outside of his family. He needed to leave his home and not feel like he was being judged."

"And you think acceptance like that is possible?"

"Absolutely. The world is changing, mostly for the better. Look at the gay community or the trans community now compared to even twenty years ago and tell me that attitudes aren't shifting in the right direction. Even something like tattoos—at one point a telltale sign of indecency, but now they're widely accepted. And I think the same strides can be made—and in some cases have been made—with mental illness."

"Why isn't this your career? Not to knock reception work or the insurance industry, but it seems like you belong there about as much as I ought to be the poster girl for the Mormons."

"That's my goal, ever since my...ever since I was fourteen."

"What's holding you back?"

She held her gaze, those piercing blue eyes seeing everything so clearly, and words died on her lips. She wasn't sure how this near stranger had been so perceptive, nor did she know how to explain the choices that had led her to her current position. Reception work had never been her idea. She hadn't even considered it until Caroline made it sound so reasonable, like the mature, responsible thing to do. Now that she was stuck in a job she hated rather than using the degree that loathsome job was helping her pay for, she felt a little foolish in retrospect. And since she was still trying to lure Eliot to the cause, she was mindful of the impression she might make.

"I probably overstepped," Eliot said. "You don't have to explain." She returned her attention to the page, her pencil in motion once again, and Harper immediately felt the loss.

"No, I want to, but it's a long story. Let's just say that the promise of a steady paycheck that would keep Sallie Mae off my back was a factor, but my goal is to work in nonprofit management. That's what I got my degree in. There just aren't many openings with the organizations I want to work with, so while I wait for something to open up, I have a boring but steady nine-to-five job. And I volunteer while I keep looking for work I want."

Eliot nodded sagely. She imagined that, as an artist, she'd probably endured her fair share of undesirable employment and understood better than anyone the tumultuous path to a dream job.

"Does that make sense? Have you ever taken a job you didn't necessarily love just to get by?"

Her sharp laugh pierced the air. "I almost always have a side job," she confessed. "And I've left most of them abruptly."

"Do you mean you've been fired?" She whispered the last word, nervous to even speak it.

"More than once. I've considered creating the world's most mundane but relatable comic book hero based on my experiences—The Terminatee."

"But, what? How?" she sputtered. Eliot didn't seem like the sort of person who would be serially dismissed. She looked like a normal woman (tattoos notwithstanding), not like someone's drunk and scraggly uncle who couldn't keep a job. And she seemed so blasé about it, like being let go was no worse than having toilet paper on your shoe. Harper had never been fired—couldn't imagine it. She'd never even gotten detention in school. She was a good person. Up until now she'd believed that only questionable people got fired.

"My mother has the same reaction every time I leave a job." She smiled easily and shrugged. "I tend to let my mouth get me into trouble because I prefer to be treated like a human being, even when I'm at work."

"You mean you've been fired for sticking up for yourself?"

"And others."

"Doesn't it scare you?"

"It would scare me more to be complacent. Besides, there's always another job."

"Especially with your bartending skills. What was that drink you made?"

"I can't reveal all my secrets."

"But how will I ever get another one if I don't know what it's called?"

"Guess you'll have to come back to my bar."

"Unless you get fired."

"Valid point." She laughed again. "So, did your girlfriend like the drink?"

"My girlfriend?"

"The pretty blonde you were with. Isn't she your girlfriend?"

"We're just friends."

"Good to know." A slow grin spread across her face, and Harper almost gasped at the glorious realization that she liked Emilia. She anticipated smooth sailing to romantic bliss for her new favorite couple.

"We should probably talk more about the fundraiser." Harper smiled broadly, her cheery, eager expression acting like a barrier between Eliot and the raw emotion she'd witnessed a moment earlier.

Reluctantly, Eliot pulled her attention away from Harper and focused again on the hasty rendering of her—the line of her cheek, her expressive brown eyes, the small cleft in her chin and her smile. All of it was breathtaking but far from her most captivating feature. She wanted to experience more of that passion, though she didn't foresee getting another glimpse before they parted ways.

"About that," Eliot stopped, suddenly not sure what to say next. Bearing the responsibility for the dimming of that smile was about as appealing as wearing fiberglass underpants. But she couldn't possibly say yes. Could she?

"Before you make up your mind, can I show you something?"

Harper's face was full of hopeful expectation, making this even harder. She knew she should say no, but instead, she checked her phone for any indication that her family needed her.

"I promise not to take up too much more of your time, unless you want to let me buy you a drink after we're done."

"Even if you don't convince me?" In spite of herself, Eliot smiled at the thought of spending more time with Harper.

"I'll buy you two drinks if you still say no. What do you say?"

She checked her dormant phone once more before answering, "I'm in."

Fifteen minutes later, Eliot stood on a busy South Loop sidewalk, staring at a building that sat on the border between historic and run-down. Still smiling, Harper escorted her inside and up to the second-floor offices of Mental Illness Allies. Like the weathered exterior of the building, Allies headquarters was in dire need of a spruce. The threadbare gray carpet had been bolstered here and there with sturdy runners, and it would be a stretch to call the workspaces anything other than functional. The desks and chairs looked like the last survivors from the dawn of office work. If not for the relatively new computers the staff used, Eliot might have believed she'd traveled back in time. Clearly the Allies budget wasn't going toward redecorating expenses.

Harper guided her down a long hallway, presumably toward the offices of the very important people running this show. As they rounded the corner, they narrowly avoided a collision with a woman who looked like the pursed-lipped, live-action version of Barbara Gordon. Unfortunately, the charming similarities seemed to end there.

As the woman teetered precariously on her heels, Harper grabbed her arm to offer support. "Phoebe, I'm so sorry."

"That's hardly the worst you've done." Phoebe scowled and removed Harper's hand from her person. "I don't suppose you have any good news for us. Or is your fundraiser still destined to sink us?"

As Harper sputtered to answer, her face flushed, whether from anger, embarrassment or a combination of the two, Eliot wasn't sure. What she did know was that Phoebe was essentially evil and that Harper needed help.

"Well, she did just recruit the artist she's been looking for."

Phoebe's eyes flicked in Eliot's direction, as if she noticed her for the first time. "I guess that's something." Her scowl lifted ever so slightly before she sauntered away.

Harper threw her arms around Eliot, catching her off guard. Harper's breath tickled her ear as she uttered the sincerest (and most oddly sensual) thanks she'd ever received. Eliot almost regretted their return to business when the embrace ended.

"I hate to ask for more from you—you're already doing so much—but I was hoping to see some of your work."

"That is a lot to ask." She winked and removed her sketchbook from her bag, handing it to Harper. She gasped as she gazed at the partial rendering of herself.

"This is wonderful."

"It's incomplete. If you'd like to see my other stuff, you can come to my apartment sometime this week and have a look."

"Would tomorrow be too soon? I can come by after work."

"Definitely not too soon." This time she was ready for the hug, just not for it to end.

CHAPTER EIGHT

Eliot stared at the ingredients assembled on her kitchen island as if that would somehow make her more suited to this task. As if merely being in the presence of flour, eggs, vanilla, and cocoa powder would transform her into the kind of person who could effortlessly whip up a delicious cake from scratch. She knew she should put this project away until later. Harper was due soon (sooner than she could hope to metamorphose into the Stan Lee of baked goods), and she didn't need to be subjected to her failed baking experiment in any of its stages.

But if she dismantled the minimal progress she'd made thus far, she doubted she'd return to the task this evening. Too many other projects demanded her attention, and every single one of them held more appeal than rekindling her relationship with her hand mixer.

Sighing at her impending baking downfall, she ditched the Cake Boss starter kit in favor of something she was undeniably good at. The mostly finished drawing of Audrey in her superhero glory sat on her desk waiting for color and a frame.

She'd intended it as a birthday gift, but with the news that Audrey would be released from the hospital in the morning, she considered turning it into a welcome home present paired with this dress rehearsal cake if she ever managed to move beyond the wishful thinking stage of baking. She could spare ten minutes to work on it before cleaning up the evidence of the Great Baking Debacle of the Decade, but knowing herself, she doubted she'd revisit the cake or its ingredients once she got wrapped up in her work.

Grabbing a rare Tuesday night drink, she settled in to make the most of what little time she had before Harper's arrival, all the while pointedly keeping her back to the cake-to-be that mocked her. She opened her case of markers and carefully selected the exact right shade of blue but got no further before her phone rang.

"How did she take it?" Alice wasted no time with pleasantries when on the hunt for information, and Eliot felt momentarily remiss for not telling her sooner about her failed charity breakup. The last time they spoke, her plan had been to dodge volunteer duty, not welcome it into her life.

"I told her yes."

"You told her yes?"

"Yes, and I'm trying to get some work done before she gets here."

"You said yes and she's coming over." Apparently Alice was going through a parrot phase. "This is not the conversation I was expecting to have, but I'm flexible. Tell me what changed your mind."

"Did you hear the part about me needing to get some work done?"

"Yes, and the sooner you talk, the sooner you can get back to that."

She spared a second she didn't have to groan. "It seems like a good cause, and she's passionate about it. And she's a decent human being so automatically easier to work with than half the population."

"She is easy on the eyes."

"That's not even remotely what I said."

"But you're also not *not* saying it."

"Just because I haven't denounced her beauty doesn't mean I'm attracted to her."

"But it doesn't mean you aren't."

"As much as I'm enjoying this conversational merry-go-round, I have to go."

"Expect a call tomorrow when you have more news to tell."

Eliot allowed herself an exasperated sigh. Dramatic, she knew, but entirely appropriate for the prospect of another probing chat about Harper and her volunteer work. She'd had a similar conversation with Georgie earlier and didn't think she had the will to survive the best friend version of that humiliation. Her sister had seemed unduly satisfied to learn that, rather than declining Harper's request for help, she'd agreed. It was almost like she'd expected such an outcome. Her knowing grin as she spoke was unbearable. She'd smirked her way through the entire conversation, as if it was a foregone conclusion that she would give in to this out-of-the-blue philanthropic request. But the bit that rankled the most was her initial comment: "She must be pretty."

Though she denied that Harper's appearance had any sway over her decision, her current eager anticipation was wildly out of proportion to the task of showing off her artwork in preparation for donating time she didn't have to a cause she didn't know existed five days ago. She wouldn't admit it to her sister or Alice, but she'd been looking forward to seeing Harper all day—not because of their plan for the evening, which was so minimal it hardly counted as an activity. She'd woken up thinking about her (a surprising treat given her moody feline alarm clock), and throughout the day, as she worked and visited with Audrey, thoughts of Harper nudged their way into her mind.

And only when the doorman called to announce she had a visitor (ten minutes early) did she realize that Harper had taken over again. She'd gotten zero work done, and her counter was still covered in traitorous provisions, but she just couldn't help the smile that took over her face.

Harper stretched and twisted to grab some kind of support as more people wedged themselves into the packed train, but she was buffeted further down the center aisle with every work-weary commuter who pressed themselves aboard the at-capacity car she found herself on. Three stops in, she'd been forced into the middle of the car, and as she clung to the overhead strap that was supposed to offer her some stability, she eyed the manspreading, seat-hogging jerk in front of her with a blend of jealousy and loathing that, with his face studiously buried in his phone and his attaché case resting comfortably on the seat beside him, he missed entirely. It was an all-too fitting end to the atrocious day she'd just endured.

From the second her workday had begun, she'd known it would be hell. How? Because she was greeted by an atypically punctual Doug lingering in the break room and looking to make small talk with any victim whose caffeine needs led them within striking distance. She honestly believed that any inanimate object would have satisfied his smarmy desire to brag about his weekend, which, by her standards, inspired about as much envy as a colonoscopy. But unlike the linoleum floor, she got to enjoy the added bonus of his creepy winks and inability to remember that her name wasn't "sweetheart." All she wanted was to top off her coffee so she could at least give the appearance of pleasantness to others, but that was out of the question once Doug opened his mouth. She retreated almost immediately, citing the required promptness of her position as the smiling face of the company, but her escape came with the clear downside of a severe caffeine deficiency.

The train lurched forward, jostling everyone around her—except for the King of Comfort himself, nose still buried in his phone. Someone's bag pressed into her lower back, and she shifted her weight from one foot to the other in a vain attempt to relieve some of the pressure on her aching feet. And just because it had been that kind of day, the cloying scent of someone's garlic breath encircled her. Even if she could free a hand to cover her nose or offer the offending party a mint, she doubted it would do much to combat the nearly tangible stink engulfing the train.

Halfway through her horrible day, she wondered if this was somehow her fault. Maybe by asking, "What else can possibly go wrong?" she'd given some capricious deity permission to answer with astounding thoroughness. Because after enduring Doug and all of his Dougliness, she'd had a minor disagreement with her least favorite IT guy, who was everyone's least favorite IT guy for good reason. She'd banged her shin on the edge of her desk, gotten her quota of papercuts for the month while tending to Floyd the intern's filing, and just to make life interesting, forgot about her lunchtime dentist appointment until ten minutes before her butt was supposed to be in the chair. Even after running the entire distance to the office, she arrived late and had to dodge the scowling judgment of the receptionist. At least she remained cavity-free, but her delayed arrival meant a tardy return, with Doug back at her desk, taking in her momentary lapse in punctuality. She ground her freshly polished teeth at the thought of the discussion he'd be sure to arrange with her over this minor infraction.

The takeaway, obviously, was just not to get out of bed in the morning, but her bank account had other opinions on that matter. And if she'd stayed in bed hiding from the world, she wouldn't be on her way to the one thing she'd been anticipating all day. The only other bright spot was the surprise text from Caroline asking if she was free for dinner that night. A weekday sighting of her girlfriend was a rare treat, but when she had to decline, the blip of happiness at the possibility quickly turned to sadness, followed immediately by guilt thanks to her disappointed reaction.

So when the train came to an abrupt halt at Wilson, signaling an end to her challenging commute, she worried that it wasn't an end to the barrage of badness the day had already assaulted her with, merely a change in venue. Her anxiety increased as she walked up to Eliot's building—a former school that had been converted into loft space. The hip factor of that alone made her feel wildly out of place, and Eliot's warm welcome did little to dispel that feeling.

She'd never been in a home that so obviously belonged to an artist. It was on the top floor and looked like some sort of minister of cool had been her interior designer. From the exposed brick walls and sliding barn doors to the ductwork and hardwood floors, the essential components of the place oozed effortless cool, and then she'd filled it with casual, comfortable-looking modern furniture, and of course, art. It made the standard two-bedroom apartment she shared with Emilia look like an emissary from Planet Uninspired.

"Can I get you something to drink?" Eliot moved toward the kitchen, turning back to look at her when Harper didn't immediately answer.

"Sure. I'll have whatever you're having," she muttered, and digging deep to find her confidence, followed her host to the kitchen. Her poise lasted all of thirty seconds before she tripped over a white cat who scurried through the room at the same time and sent her stumbling directly into Eliot's arms.

"I'm sorry my cat just tried to kill you." She held on to her until she regained her footing (though not her composure). "You obviously weren't paying him the proper attention."

"Clearly assassination was in order." She took a half step back, and, trying to hide her embarrassment, she bent to pet the feline cause of her most recent klutziness. "He's awfully cute for an attempted murderer."

"Don't encourage him. He's already insufferable."

He blinked demurely at her, a clear display of innocence, though his one eye made it seem like he was conspiring with her rather than convincing her of his harmlessness. She felt Eliot's eyes on her as she doted on the cat, and knowing that, after her stellar entry, she didn't have the confidence to meet Eliot's gaze, she turned away when she rose from her brief stint as feline assassin tamer. That's when she noticed the countertop had been overrun by an alarming array of baking staples. It was like Emilia had taken over the kitchen.

She gestured at the ingredient squad. "What's all this?"

"A birthday cake." She looked from Eliot to her counter, back again and blinked in confusion. "Some assembly required."

"There are easier ways to get your dessert fix."

"All of them guaranteed to horrify my mother."

"How will she know? Does she have regular communication with the good people at Sara Lee?"

"I'm in charge of the cake for my niece's birthday party, and if I even contemplate bringing something as impersonal and flavorless as a mass-produced cake, I'll secure my standing as the greatest living source of maternal disappointment. This year especially."

"What's so important about this year?"

"My niece has cancer."

"I'm so sorry."

"No, I'm sorry. I could have eased you into that."

"Is she okay?"

"She will be. I think. We just found out she gets to leave the hospital tomorrow, which means she'll be home for her birthday this weekend. Hence the high-pressure cake."

"What if you bought it from the absolute best baker in the city, possibly the entire Midwest?"

"I take it you know this person?"

"She's only my best friend—the pretty blonde you met on Saturday, and she's amazing." She couldn't believe the golden matchmaking opportunity that had just been handed to her. "She's also my roommate and sometimes my boss. I'm there a lot, allegedly helping her but really just getting in her way. And trying not to gain three hundred pounds. I might even be able to convince her to make it look less than perfect, just to throw your mother off the scent of professional baking."

"I'll be forever in your debt if you can pull that off."

"Or you could volunteer your services at my very important fundraiser, and we can call it even." She texted a link to the bakery's website and smiled at her skillful matchmaking opportunism. Everything was working out perfectly.

"That seems fair."

Eliot couldn't help staring at Harper's smile. Just like the woman herself, it was charming and inviting and something she wanted to see more of. And though neither of them seemed eager to break their lingering gaze, they had work to do.

"Let me fix you that drink." Harper nodded slowly, still not looking away. "I put some samples of my work on the coffee table. Feel free to take a look."

She nodded again, and after checking to see that her path was Scott-free, moved to the other room. Eliot tried hard not to watch as she walked away, but she looked so good doing it. Still, she didn't want to be a creep (or worse, be caught acting like one), so reluctantly, she tore her eyes away from the view and forced herself to focus on something other than her guest's backside.

As she busied herself with pouring drinks, she wondered how she might convince her to stick around after all the art talk was finished. Once that was over, what was the likelihood they'd need to meet again? True, they had cake subterfuge to arrange, but that would only last until the weekend. What if this was the last time she'd see her until the fundraiser? That was too long to wait. She could draw out this process, but she'd rather spend their time together doing something more fun. And just like that, several images of fun she could have with Harper filled her mind.

"Um, Eliot." Harper saved her from her thoughts. "All I see on the coffee table is an irritated cat and a couple stacks of comic books. Am I missing something?"

"Nope." She joined her on the couch and placed a drink in her hand. If she had a bigger ego, she might have been bothered that she was so clueless about her work. Instead, she found it oddly endearing.

She grabbed a book from the stack and opened it to her favorite panel. In it, the heroine struggled to overpower her enemy—a brute mutant who was seconds from crushing her. It had taken forever to render her facial expression with the right blend of determination and dread—so long she almost questioned her career path. But by the time the inker and colorist had finished with it, it was a stunning, powerful reminder of why she'd been drawn to this job. She loved both the solitary nature of the work and the collaborative efforts that brought it all together. Not that Harper got that much from the page she stared at.

"You drew this?" She held the book almost reverently, as if it was an ancient artifact or a priceless relic rather than one issue of many in a long-running series.

"And this, this and this." She pointed to several other panels in that book before grabbing the next one in the stack. "I drew everything in this one and handled all the inking but not the coloring. And in this one," she pulled a book from the other stack, "I did everything except write it."

"You drew this?" she asked again, her gaze still riveted to the first book she held.

"Among other things. But my work is represented in this entire stack."

"I had no idea." She carefully turned the pages of the top book—the first in *The Scarlet Avenger* series. "I can't believe I'm in the same room as a verified comic nerd."

"Do you always treat your volunteers with such reverence and respect?"

"Of course. It's why they're so devoted to me and my cause."

"That and the promise of cake."

"Exactly. Now back to you being a comic book nerd. Aren't you too cool for that?"

"Are you questioning my comic street cred?"

"I am, especially now that I've seen where you live. Your fortress of solitude doesn't really reflect your secret identity as a comics nerd. Shouldn't there be pictures of Wonder Woman adorning your walls? At least a refrigerator magnet or two?"

"No disrespect to Diana Prince, but I'm a Kate Bishop girl, and yes, you will find the full collection of Hawkeye comics beside my bed," she huffed. Wonder Woman was great and all, recent disappointing Hollywood adaptation of her life notwithstanding, but she was beyond an obvious choice.

"I'm no longer doubting your nerd status."

"Thank you. So, do I have the job?" she asked, softening her tone.

"I don't know. Do you really think my little organization is worthy of your talents?"

"I think you sell your little organization and yourself short. And you shouldn't." Harper cast her eyes downward, and a bashful grin spread across her face. Eliot was drawn to her vulnerability, and she realized she was unconsciously moving toward Harper's full lips. "Are you hungry?" she asked, surprising herself.

"Starving, but considering what I've learned about your culinary skills, I'm not sure I trust you to do anything about that."

"I wasn't suggesting we have cake for dinner, but it's probably safer if we go out."

An easy grin appeared, and their eyes locked once more. "That's probably our best option."

CHAPTER NINE

Eliot wasn't sure of the exact nature of this outing. Dinner could be interpreted in a number of ways, and while she had clear ideas of where she'd like this dinner to be headed, she couldn't exactly call it a date. For one thing, dates were special, particularly first dates. They weren't addendums to a business meeting. And the restaurant they were heading to, while one of her favorites, likely wouldn't be considered special to anyone who didn't have the rich history with it that she had. Beyond the fairly mundane nature of the evening so far, it hadn't been officially declared a date. She didn't necessarily need that designation in writing, but spoken aloud might be nice. She wanted to have more than wishful thinking and prolific flirting to go on.

Glancing at Harper, who, despite the ample width of the sidewalk they traversed, walked close enough that a gnat would find it challenging to pass between them, she got the strong impression that she wasn't alone in her optimistic conclusion. They'd wrapped up their business quickly, yet neither of them seemed eager for their time together to end. She hadn't hesitated to say yes to dinner, which could be explained by extreme hunger. However, that could have been addressed more quickly by stopping at any of the nearby diners or fast food chains after bidding her farewell. They'd passed no fewer than three places to grab a quick bite as they made their way to Ida's, and any one of them would have satisfied her appetite. Opting for a sit-down meal with her over the instant gratification of a Big Mac implied that hunger was only one factor in her decision, and not the most important one.

Still, she felt bad that the poor girl had to walk five blocks past restaurant after restaurant just to get to Ida's for a could-be date in a restaurant that was emphatically platonic and about as far from fine dining as a dining place could get. Worse, she had no idea where they were going. For all she knew this was the mealtime equivalent of the Bataan Death March, and six days later she'd still be starving.

"I promise it's not that much farther."

"Am I complaining?" The meager grin that appeared captured none of her usual radiance, but she attributed that to hunger exacerbated by physical exertion.

"No. You're not saying anything, which in my brief experience with you is rare."

"Hey!" Harper nudged her shoulder with her own. "You make it seem like it's a bad thing that I'm friendly, and by the way, I can be a lot less friendly if you'd prefer."

Eliot guessed the expression she offered was supposed to be menacing, but it came out a lot closer to adorable. "Oh, I have no problem with your current level of friendliness." She winked (according to her sister, that was her superpower) and tried not to dwell on what had Harper so distracted.

Harper had been quiet for good reason. As soon as they set out for the restaurant that Eliot swore was worth the seemingly endless walk from her apartment, a wave of guilt had washed over her. She realized belatedly that she should have checked with Caroline first. Not for permission, but because of her earlier invitation. It was hardly considerate that she said no to her girlfriend because she didn't have time, but now that she had time, she was traipsing halfway across the neighborhood with someone else. Shouldn't she spend time with her girlfriend rather than running off with another woman?

Though she supposed it was fair, considering that Caroline had spent the entire weekend doing just that. Not the running off with another woman part, of course, but canceling plans and generally being unavailable. She'd prioritized their relationship below every other consideration on the planet, so she could hardly complain now that she was getting a glimpse of what Harper experienced regularly since their relationship began.

Hearing echoes of Emilia in her last thought, she opted to shut down her internal commentary and simply enjoy her present company.

The restaurant was the diametric opposite of Eliot's apartment, at least on the cool meter. There were crisp linens on the tables and adorably kitschy moo-cow creamers. It looked like a restaurant her grandmother might have opened, if her grandmother's skills in the kitchen had extended beyond remembering to put the milk out with the cereal. Eliot looked eight hundred and five percent out of place in such a quaint setting with its lacy curtains and air of antiquity, but she obviously hadn't been lying about loving this spot.

The hostess, who clearly predated the restaurant—possibly all restaurants—offered a warm, if feeble, hug and admonished Eliot for staying away so long. Her greeting was laced with the charming blend of irascibility and tenderness particular to ladies of her generation.

"Ida, it's only been two weeks, and you know why I haven't been in." She planted a gentle kiss on the papery skin of the old woman's cheek before escaping from her lingering embrace.

"Even more reason for you to come by. With all that little girl is going through, at the very least she deserves a bowl of my soup. I'll pack up some chicken noodle for you to take to her." She continued her rebuke as she showed them to their table.

Her pace being rather closer to tortoise than hare, by the time they reached their destination, they'd both gotten an earful.

The booth was as uncomfortable as it looked, its hard vinyl upholstery squeaking but not yielding with their weight. Fortunately, it wasn't cracked, but it was a bit like trying to get comfortable on molded concrete. The spotless tabletop was worn and scarred, likely because of the countless diners and thorough cleanings it had endured since its debut during the Great War.

"You tell that sister of yours she's in even more trouble. Forgetting all about an old woman. I'm creeping closer to the grave without so much as a hello from her."

"You're immortal, Ida, but I'll make sure she comes by soon."

"You're full of surprises," Harper said as she watched the woman totter away, as much out of fascination as concern for her safety.

Ida hadn't made it halfway back to the hostess stand when a geriatric waitress shuffled up to them and turned her rheumy eyes on Eliot. "So you finally decided to come check on an old lady. Glad to know I rank so high on your list."

She rose and hugged the old woman, whose giant smile conveyed her true feelings. "I'm sorry I haven't visited lately, but you know why I haven't been around as much."

"And how is that little niece of yours? Any better?" She offered a noncommittal shrug. "You tell her we have chocolate milk and a bottomless sundae for her the next time she visits."

"You just made her year with an offer like that. Thank you, Faye." They hugged again before she resumed her seat, her easy grin firmly in place as Harper looked from her to the waitress and back again. She wanted to offer the woman her seat, or better yet, take over her shift.

Sooner than she thought possible, Faye returned with two drinks and plates of steaming food they hadn't ordered. Understandable since she'd never even seen a menu or been acknowledged beyond a casual, "How you doin', hon?" from Faye. She seemed to know without asking what Eliot wanted and apparently assumed Harper would like the same thing.

Not that she minded the peculiar attention. It was sort of fun to have a surprise dinner, but she wondered what they would do when confronted with allergies. She almost wanted to feign one just to see what would happen, but that would probably backfire on her. The next time she came here with Eliot, she'd be locked into whatever foods fit her pretend limitations, and she might miss out. And then she realized she was imagining subsequent dinners with Emilia's future girlfriend, which weren't likely unless they double dated. She didn't need to contemplate the likelihood of Caroline and Em getting along for the length of a meal (even one as fast, and based on her first bite, delicious as this) to know it would never work.

"Out of curiosity, have you ever ordered on your own, or do they always just decide what you want and hope for the best?"

"Maybe once when I was fifteen."

"I guess it's a lot like meals when I was younger. Mom would pretty much decide the menu based on what she felt like cooking. We could make requests, and she was generally pretty accommodating, especially for Blake."

She smiled at the memory of her brother sweet talking their mom into cooking his favorite foods—lasagna in the sweltering heat of July or nutrient sparse grilled cheese for his birthday. She almost never told him no, even when his requests meant an extra trip to the store. And though her mom rarely denied either of her children if she could help it, Blake always had a better track record with her.

"Everything okay?" The question snapped her out of her memory.

"Fine." She attempted a smile and turned her attention to the food she'd been pushing around her plate for who knew how long.

"You don't have to be."

"What do you mean?"

"You tend to disappear when you talk about your brother. I don't know exactly what happened to him, but if what I think happened did, that's not something you have to be fine about, at least not with me." Her expression was curious but kind, like she was genuinely interested but wouldn't push for information that Harper didn't want to give. It was oddly comforting.

"What do you think happened?"

Usually she sidestepped this conversation. People wanted to know the details out of morbid curiosity or to satisfy some warped need for gossip. How it affected her was secondary to their pretend concern. But something about the kindness in those blue eyes and the way Eliot had asked made her think that, maybe, she was safe.

"Did he commit suicide?"

She nodded, unable to speak around the lump in her throat.

"He must have been young."

"Nineteen." Her voice barely above a whisper, she cleared her throat and tried again. "He was nineteen, and I was fourteen, and I—" She couldn't finish that statement, couldn't blurt out over a heaping mound of mac and cheese the brutal truth of finding her big brother lifeless in his room, of how she'd foolishly tried to save him and just made everything worse. "I think I'd rather talk about something happier."

"I think that's a good idea," Eliot said and instantly shifted gears, telling her all about Ida, Faye and her history with the place where they sat enjoying an unexpectedly delicious meal of comfort food. By the time Faye cleared their plates, Eliot had gotten her much closer to laughter than tears.

"This is actually where I had my first job," she told Harper as she paid the bill, refusing to let her even contribute to the tip.

"I'm guessing it ended better than the rest of your jobs."

"I wasn't fired, if that's what you're suggesting."

"You can't blame me for thinking that. You've been fired a lot."

"So, so many times."

They were walking toward the train, enjoying the cool night air. It smelled of spring and impending rain, and she wanted to linger in the combined glow of the street lamps and half-moon.

"Thank you for tonight."

"Anytime."

They gravitated toward each other as they passed into the shadow of a building a group of hyperactive teens emerged from, and Eliot slowed her pace. The darkness enveloped them, and for a moment, everything was still—no cars zooming past, their mufflers and radios competing for attention, no raucous kids out for fun or mayhem. Just the two of them sharing an extraordinary moment of silence. She was about to marvel at the quiet when Eliot stopped and turned to her.

Time slowed as she leaned closer, their lips almost touching, her eyes searching Harper's. Their breath mingled in their closeness, and there was a brief pause, the barest hesitation before their lips met. She found herself falling into the moment, allowing herself to escape in the softness of her lips, the gentle urgency of her tongue. She savored the sweetness of the contact, of Eliot's hand on the small of her back, drawing her closer, of her other hand linking fingers with hers and the soft, sighing moan that escaped as she pressed herself against her. She could get lost in this moment, she thought, and then she realized how thoroughly she had. Her next thought was of Caroline, who she should have been thinking of exclusively, all night long. Not to mention Emilia. Eliot was supposed to be for her, so why was she the one being kissed?

As the weight of what happened dawned on her, she jumped back, and without another word, ran from Eliot.

CHAPTER TEN

Hindsight wasn't twenty-twenty—it was a goddamn high-powered microscope that magnified every second that Harper would rather not relive. No matter what she did to forget the kiss (and she'd tried everything short of a fishbowl-sized serving of tequila and an anvil to the head), every time she closed her eyes, she went right back to that charged moment on the sidewalk when the universe decided that her life just wasn't complicated enough.

She sensed it in the moment just before the kiss happened. She'd be completely naïve if she hadn't. Their entire evening had been such a build-up to it that only a fool would believe their time together could end in anything other than a kiss. And even when she'd known what Eliot's plans were, she'd done nothing to dissuade her. Worse, she'd ushered it in. She'd practically put out a welcome mat. She could admit now (when it was too late to take precautionary measures) the intense pull she felt toward her. She'd been curious. How could she not be? She was unlike anyone she had met before. But did that really warrant a public make-out session? Her conscience said no, but her lips obviously disagreed.

Once her brain caught up with the rest of her body, she'd done the only logical thing she could do—run away without explanation.

Eliot called after her, of course, but the longing in her voice just made her pick up her pace. She was practically sprinting by the time she reached the el station, and she refused to turn around and look, fearful of what she would see, whether Eliot had followed her or not. If she looked back and saw her there, breathless and flushed, she would undoubtedly do something she would regret—more than she already had. But if she turned around and didn't find her? If she hadn't come after her, if she'd simply let her go into the night, that would be worse, especially since it's what she should hope for. She had a girlfriend—a girlfriend she admired and loved—and had no business kissing anyone else or wishing she could do it again.

She was the worst girlfriend on the planet.

And she wasn't a very good friend either. Not that Emilia had been happily on board with the intended pairing between her and Eliot, but she'd eventually come around. And now when she did, things would be awkward because she'd kissed her best friend's true love.

She ignored the fact that Eliot's skillful kissing of her was a fairly clear indication that she wasn't Em's true love. One kiss didn't have to ruin everything, and if Eliot had someone more available on whom to focus her considerable lip work, it would be better for everyone. She had no reason (other than a toe-curling kiss) to believe her feelings for her were more than fleeting interest. To ensure that nothing further developed, she realized she needed to double down on pairing Eliot up with Emilia. She suddenly wished she had been brave enough to look back—not for her own satisfaction, but to have a better idea of what she was dealing with.

The insistent buzz of her phone roused her from her thoughts, but when she saw that it was Eliot calling, she let it go to voice mail. She wasn't ready to face the situation yet—not because she didn't want to explain about her girlfriend (thus eliminating any future kissing). She just needed time to think. She needed to process what had happened and figure out how to deal with it before she talked to anyone.

The evening hadn't ended quite the way Eliot had intended. She thought Harper would respond well to the kiss. And she had at first. She'd unquestionably reciprocated, but then, like a switch had flipped, she'd fled the scene without looking back. She hadn't necessarily expected the kiss to turn into a trip back to her bedroom, but she had hoped it would progress to more advanced kissing. That was the grade school version of kissing Harper. She wanted a PhD.

But instead of being breathless from making out with a beautiful woman, she'd ended up winded from her ultimately futile pursuit of an apparent master of mixed signals. She'd tried calling her but got no answer. The message she left was apologetic and admittedly confused, but she had no way of gauging how the recently mercurial Harper would take it. Who knew? She might really enjoy it at first and then run away from her phone.

But she needed to talk to someone, and beyond sprawling across her lap and drifting off to sleep, Scott had made his disinterest in her problems known. Sighing, she picked up her phone and hoped she wouldn't regret what she was about to do.

"I hate peach," Georgie answered on the first ring. "Who decided on that color for hospital rooms? It's not soothing for anyone who has to look at it for more than fifteen seconds. And after three days, it's full-on aggravating. I'm thinking of lodging a complaint with the administrators. There might be a petition involved."

"Things are going well at the hospital I take it."

"We're all a little restless, counting the hours until we get to go home."

"Well, maybe I can distract you. Do you have time to handle a dilemma?"

"I do have an anti-peach campaign to mount, but I can take a few minutes to fix your life. Hit me."

"Is there ever a good explanation for a woman to run away from someone who kissed her?"

"Who did you kiss?"

"That's probably not important since she didn't exactly respond in an encouraging way. She's not likely to come back for more anytime soon."

"I reluctantly acknowledge your point."

"So, did I ruin everything?"

"I will need a little more to go on than the bare minimum you've given me. What preceded the kiss?"

"Showing off my comic book genius and dinner at Ida's." She could almost feel Georgie's impatient glower through the phone, so she filled in the details, from their meeting on Friday all the way up to the unfortunate lip lock on Wilson Avenue.

"You've known her five days, and you're already going for PDA? You know that's not what they mean by speed dating, right?"

"There is a reason I've had a zillion girlfriends since high school."

"But you're using a lifeline on this girl? You like her, don't you."

"As a rule I don't go around kissing women I don't like."

"Don't play dumb. You like this one more than usual, so you've turned to your less worldly but more knowledgeable little sister for advice."

Georgie excelled at gloating, possibly thanks to the ample opportunities afforded her by her big sister.

"Don't be ridiculous. It's only been five days, remember? Apparently I shouldn't even be kissing her, let alone feeling things for her."

"Because that's how love works."

"Just forget I called. I'll see you tomorrow when we will absolutely not be discussing this."

"Don't be so sensitive," she relented. "It certainly sounds like she was giving you the green light. Maybe you're a bad kisser. Have you ever had any complaints?"

"Do you really want the answer to that question?"

"About as much as I want to think about my parents' sex life."

"Just assume it wasn't the kissing. Why would she run away?"

"I'm not really the person who can answer that."

"She didn't answer when I called."

"I'd say try again. You're never going to know what's going on if you rely on speculation, especially from your sister who's never even met—what was her name again?"

"Nice try."

CHAPTER ELEVEN

"How did your art thing go? Can she draw?"

Em's amused interest managed to distract her only briefly from measuring ingredients for her cinnamon rolls. The store wouldn't open for another twenty minutes, and the relative calm before the morning rush was deceptively peaceful.

"It was fine. She's, um, a really good artist." Harper helped herself to some of the bakery's freshly brewed coffee and worked to turn her mood from sullen guilt to enthusiastic matchmaker. Despite the conflicts she now knew were facing this pairing, she still believed it was the right thing to do—for even more reasons. Not only would it help her friend, at least in theory, but it would also help Harper wash away her guilty feelings. Best of all, it would send a clear message to Eliot (and anyone else who might eventually learn of the kiss) that she wasn't interested. Not at all. Her loyalties were to Caroline and Emilia, and no amount of earth-shattering, breath-taking, mind-blowing kissing would change that.

Which was why it was so frustrating that, apparently, it was all she could think about. Even when she tried to redirect her attention to her girlfriend, Eliot and her lips were right there in her memory, making her feel ashamed. She shook her head, wishing her mind was like an Etch A Sketch. She'd love to wipe away the last ten hours or at least pretend that the last five minutes of her otherwise delightful evening with Eliot had never happened.

"What are you thinking about?" Em was leaning against the counter, flour coating her hands and apron, a concerned expression clouding her face.

"I was thinking about Eliot and you."

"If that's the look you get on your face when you contemplate us as a couple, I think we should stick with my plan of avoiding it."

"But she likes you."

"Really? Because all evidence I've seen points to the contrary."

"She called you pretty."

"I say flowers are pretty all the time. Doesn't mean I should strike up a relationship with a hydrangea the next time I see one."

"She said it when she was checking to see if you were my girlfriend. And she's planning on visiting the bakery soon." All of those statements were technically true. She didn't need to know that she'd orchestrated the meeting at the bakery or that Eliot's interest was in her, at least until she could redirect it.

"Just to see little old me?"

"And to buy a cake for her niece's birthday."

"Sounds like true love. I'm flattered."

"If it's meant to be, it doesn't matter how things start."

"But if it's meant to be, do you really need to keep pushing it?"

"Maybe that's how the universe is working this out. I'm just a tool of fate."

"Why is this so important to you?" At the beep of the timer, Emilia was back to work, but not finished with this conversation.

"I just want you to be happy."

"Except that I've told you repeatedly that this isn't what I want. This is making me the opposite of happy, but you keep ignoring that. Not that you're not normally adorably insistent, but this is bordering on extreme. What's really going on?"

Though she ought to have found some comfort in talking to her best friend's back rather than maintaining eye contact, she really just wanted to avoid the conversation entirely.

"I do think you guys would make a great couple."

"But?" At the hint of a twist in the story, she offered her full attention, making this even more difficult.

"But I guess Eliot thought she and I would make a great couple." She offered a combination shrug-wince-grimace that she hoped would sell her blamelessness. "She might have kissed me last night."

"When will you be sure?"

She allowed herself one exasperated sigh before sharing the details of her night. "I took way too long to stop her, so long that if not for the part where I ran from her, she probably thinks I liked it."

Em shook her head and ceased all baking activity. "There's so much to unpack here, not the least of which is you deciding to dump your cast-off suitors on me." She opened her mouth to explain, but Em shut her down. "We'll talk about that later. Right now I'm going to risk making you as mad at me as I am at you. I know you don't want to hear this, but I think she's right. You two would make a good couple."

"How can you possibly say that?"

"Why didn't you stop her right away?"

"I was surprised."

"And? You're also surprised when you step in Mary Berry's hairballs, but you don't stand there for five minutes letting it squish between your toes. I think you liked the kiss."

"Did not." Not even she found her lie believable.

"Admit it. You liked the kiss and you like her."

"I don't know where you're getting that from."

"Because I've seen the two of you together, remember? You're basing our compatibility on the convenient fact that

Eliot and I are both single. I'm basing my opinion on a well-documented history of flirtation and comparing the way she looked at you versus how she looked at every other woman in that bar."

"But I'm with Caroline."

"And Caroline's with her job."

"You know what? I don't want to talk about this anymore. I have to get to work."

She stormed out of the kitchen, lamenting the fact that it was impossible to satisfy her anger with the unslammable swinging door.

While cute and cozy, the bakery didn't really look like it would be her salvation. Taking up the bottom half of a two-story brick building, its no-frills interior looked to Eliot more or less like every other bakery she'd ever seen. True, the splashes of bright color throughout gave it a little more character than the standard pastry-pushing establishment. This seemed like it might be a fun place to stop in if she weren't worried about a possible hostile reception, but it also seemed to offer pretty much what any bakery could offer. Based on visuals alone, Segatti's Bakery was a slightly more fun take on a fairly standard concept.

Adding to the bakery's charm, the worn tables lining the outer edge of the space looked like they'd survived more than one dining skirmish and weren't prepared to give up any time soon. She could easily envision them taking up a corner at Ida's, and she instantly fell a little in love with the place. The cash register was even older, which was sort of charming in a perplexing way. She didn't see any means for credit card or electronic payments but hoped Harper's friend had accommodated for the demands of the modern world. While she herself had a great fondness for cash, she didn't see how any establishment in this day could survive being cash only.

Behind the counter, which was as well-worn as the tables, a swinging door obviously led to the kitchen, where the alleged magic happened. With no real evidence, she guessed that it was as gleaming but dated as the rest of the place and wondered if Harper's friend (who appeared to be as young as Harper herself) had shunned modernity out of necessity, or if there was a practical reason for her lack of upgrades? Certainly remodeling and updating would be pricey. But maybe there was another reason. Perhaps food just tasted better when it came with a visual association with simpler times and sweet grandmothers. Or possibly she believed that the quality of her product made up for the antiquated package it came in. If that was the case, then she probably had nothing to worry about, at least where the cake was concerned.

She recognized Emilia, the ostensible baking genius, as she breezed through the door, her arms laden with trays of admittedly tempting foods, her determination and satisfaction evident. Rather than the party clothes she'd worn to the bar, today she sported jeans, a plain white T-shirt and an apron. A red bandanna covered her hair, and a smudge of flour dotted her cheek. Like Rosie the Riveter of the kitchen, she exuded confidence, offering some reassurance that she wasn't continuing a long series of mistakes by ordering Audrey's cake from this place. But she'd never know if she loitered on the curb rather than going in to get what she came for (or at least one of the things she came for).

Emilia glanced up at the jingle of the bell over the door, but the look she gave Eliot was closer to tolerant than happy to see a potential paying customer patronizing her sparsely populated store. Eliot wasn't sure if that was because she had background information that affected her opinion, or if Emilia merely didn't grasp the connection between good customer service and the bottom line. Determined to go through with this no matter how uncomfortable it might get, she offered what she hoped was a charming smile, eliciting a negligible grin in return. After sizing her up, Emilia made actual eye contact, the kind that connected rather than just flicking in the general vicinity of her eyes. Progress.

"What brings you in?"

"I need a cake."

"I suspected as much."

"What gave me away? Do I look like a cake fiend?"

"There are certain signs. And Harper told me you might be coming in."

Eliot wondered what else Harper had said. "Is she here?" She glanced around the shop eagerly, as if she somehow missed her lurking in a corner or hiding under a table.

"No." Based on that terse response, she wouldn't be volunteering more information, but it couldn't make things any worse if she asked.

"Do you expect her to come in?"

"It doesn't seem likely. She was pretty upset when she left this morning."

Her heart sank. Not only because she'd now fruitlessly exhausted all of her options to make things right, but also because she had no idea she could do so much damage with one kiss.

"Do you still want the cake?" That was all she was going to get out of Emilia, it seemed, but this didn't have to be an entirely wasted trip.

"That depends. I basically want a miracle in edible form. You can do that, right?"

"It's my bread and butter. And I do mean that literally."

After explaining her situation and Harper's enthusiastic suggestion that Emilia was exactly what she needed to satisfy her niece and keep her mother's judgment mostly at bay, they got down to business, discussing the particulars of the dessert that would be her redemption. While she knew that, from her mother's perspective, it was implausible at best that she had pulled off a triple-layer chocolate chip cake with green buttercream frosting and wombat decorations, she knew Audrey would love it, and that was really all that mattered. It wasn't like her relationship with her mother could get any worse.

Even after finalizing the order and paying, she still held out hope of running into Harper. It was undoubtedly foolish and probably a little masochistic, but she couldn't help thinking that, if she just got the chance to talk to her, she could set things right. So, in part to kill time and in part out of genuine pastry lust, she stood eyeing the donuts in the case. Like Sirens on the shores of the Land of Bad Carbs, they called to her. They were like the kind of donuts that regular donuts aspired to be. Responsible Eliot (who had been notoriously quiet of late) suggested she consider something more appropriate for an adult at dinnertime, but Ligeia of the pastry case squelched that argument. It wouldn't hurt to get a couple, just to help gauge Emilia's baking abilities. And she thought Audrey would probably enjoy a treat. She didn't want to show up to her niece's triumphant dehospitalization empty-handed.

"You're allowed to buy them. You don't have to restrict yourself to staring at them." Without waiting for her to respond, Emilia extracted a chocolate glazed donut from the case and passed it to her. "I usually run out of these by noon. You're lucky it was a slow morning."

She had no idea that eating a donut could be a transformative experience, but from the first bite, she wanted to renounce all other foods, even her mother's spinach manicotti.

"I want to have its children," she moaned as soon as she swallowed.

"Only if I can sell them."

"Seems fair." She winked and offered to take the rest of the donuts off her hands.

"She was upset with me, by the way," Emilia said as she boxed the pastries. "Harper."

"Did you kiss her, too?" She probably shouldn't have said that, but Emilia's sharp crack of laughter reassured her.

"No. But I did tell her she'd be better off kissing you than her girlfriend."

The small space reeled around her as an unfathomable blend of clarity and confusion took over and spun her worldview.

"She has a girlfriend?"

"For the past twelve unbearable months."

"I had no idea."

"I have to say I'm surprised but relieved to hear that. I didn't really want to encourage my best friend to consider dating a woman who went around kissing people in relationships."

Just when it seemed impossible that Eliot hadn't reached the apex of her confusion, Em dropped a bombshell like that. "The girlfriend's that bad?"

"Yes, but I also think maybe you're that good."

"Thanks for the vote of confidence. Doesn't seem to have worked, though. She's pretty aggressively ignoring me."

"I'll see what I can do about that."

"You don't need to get involved."

"Call it self-preservation." She raised her eyebrows in a question. "Long story that I hope we can laugh about later. And," she said as she handed over her sinful wares, "she works on the weekends, Saturday mornings in particular."

"Thanks, Emilia."

CHAPTER TWELVE

"Your new girlfriend stopped in today."

"She's not my girlfriend."

"Then how did you know who I was talking about?"

"Must have been your lack of subtlety," Harper grumbled and kept quiet about seeing Eliot through the window and immediately turning the other direction. Nor did she admit she admired Eliot's ass before her retreat. She didn't want to give Em any more ammunition for the argument she'd made that morning (and that she'd tried not to think about all day).

"Don't you want to know how it went?"

She shrugged her indifference and waited for the details. Though she wanted to avoid the topic of her and Eliot, she was dying to know if Eliot and Em had fallen instantly in love as she'd intended.

"I think she'll be ecstatic with the cake."

"Of course she will be. Did you talk about anything else?"

"We may have touched on some other topics."

"Such as?"

"Donuts."

"Wow. Sounds like you really hit it off. When is the wedding announcement?"

"I'll try to squeeze it in somewhere between winning the lottery and becoming president."

"You're not even a little bit interested in her?"

"It wouldn't matter if I was."

She felt her face grow hot under Em's pointed gaze but managed not to squirm.

"We also talked about you, in particular your girlfriend, who she didn't even know existed."

"That doesn't excuse her just randomly kissing people."

"She kissed you, not people, and I doubt it was all that random. I think she had good reason to believe you were open to being kissed."

"I never suggested anything of the kind."

"Based on what I witnessed when we saw her at the bar, I'm surprised she waited so long. More importantly, you didn't tell her you had a girlfriend."

"That shouldn't be the only information that prevents someone from planting one on you, should it?"

"Not my point. I'm wondering how, in the admittedly brief time you've known her, she didn't know about Caroline."

"It just never came up."

"Please. Last week I was telling you about the new aprons I ordered, and somehow we ended up discussing the lease on Caroline's BMW. In the last year, she has managed to make a guest appearance in almost every conversation we've ever had."

"Not true."

"True enough. I hear about her no fewer than five times a day, and I suspect that if I wasn't a hostile audience, I'd get an even fuller ear than I already do. So how did Eliot, who hasn't met Caroline and therefore has no reason to hate her, not know that the love of your life existed?"

Harper replayed her encounters with Eliot, and while it was true that the subject of Caroline hadn't directly come up at any point that she could remember, she knew she'd had ample opportunity to mention her. Like when they'd met for coffee practically at the doorstep of her work. Or when Eliot had asked if Em was her girlfriend, or when she'd questioned her choice of jobs. At any point in their interactions, she could have dropped a few hints that she wasn't single. And since Em was right about her tendency to insinuate Caroline into conversations whenever the opportunity presented itself (or even when it didn't), Harper now had the same questions as Em. How had she never mentioned Caroline? She was proud of her work and her, so she talked about her, perhaps more than others appreciated. Yet when it came to Eliot, she hadn't even suggested that she existed. While she wouldn't go so far as to say that she intentionally misled Eliot, she surely hadn't been entirely forthright.

"I don't know. Maybe I liked having somebody who didn't keep trying to tell me how terrible my girlfriend is."

"And it doesn't bother you that you only got that because she didn't know Caroline existed?"

"You can't know that's the only reason."

"And you can't know it isn't."

She glared, but the effect was lost on her back as Emilia disappeared into the kitchen.

She returned shortly with two glasses of wine and her serious conversation expression firmly in place. "I have a perfectly reasonable explanation that you're sure to hate and deny." She paused long enough for both of them to sip their wine, and then she uttered the most ridiculous sentence imaginable. "You like Eliot."

"I do not."

"Okay, except you do." She held up a hand to stop whatever protest Harper was about to make. "You don't want to admit it because you think being attracted to someone somehow makes you a bad person. But it's there, and if you make me offer proof, I will. And because you like her, you wanted her to like you, too. It worked, by the way. And to be clear, I'm not judging you. Eliot is attractive, about a thousand times more attractive than Caroline based on personality alone. And even if she wasn't, you can't help what you feel."

"But I can help how I behave, and I behaved badly."

"Not as badly as you're beating yourself up for. You should give yourself a break, and you should talk to Eliot. She's feeling pretty bad and should get the full explanation from you. I'd say you owe her that much."

"What do I tell Caroline?"

"You tell her nothing."

"I can't lie to her."

"You already have. Why change now?"

"Because she deserves the truth."

"Pretend for a minute that she told you another woman kissed her. She stopped it, even though she was attracted to that woman, but she promised nothing more would happen because she was trying to pawn her admirer off on her best friend. How much are you loving that honesty now?"

"I see your point, but I'm only in this mess because of a similar dishonesty. I don't see how a more convenient omission of facts will help the situation."

"You know what? Don't take my word for it. If you really don't believe me, ask her how she would feel about someone else kissing you. I'm guessing it won't get rave reviews."

"So I just do nothing?"

"No. You think about why you really feel guilty about this. Think about how you would have reacted if Caroline wasn't in the picture. Since you love honesty so much, don't be afraid to be honest with yourself. Ask yourself what you truly want, and if that's not enough, talk to your mother about it."

She sighed, knowing Em was right—at least about needing to figure out what she wanted—but not really wanting to try any of it. She wasn't saying she agreed about her and Eliot making a good couple, but she owed it to Caroline (and Eliot, she admitted) to spend at least as much time considering the situation as she had running away from all thoughts about it. And once she'd done that, she could purge all thoughts of Eliot from her mind. It wouldn't be easy, but it was the right thing to do.

"Fine. Anything else?"

"Yeah. Stop trying to set me up with your girlfriend."

"She's not my girlfriend."

She supposed it was naive of her to expect Audrey to look suddenly healthy just because she'd traded a hospital bed for her own. She may have improved enough to come home, but it wasn't like she'd left her cancer behind. Still, Eliot's cheeks were starting to ache from so much smiling at the sight of her niece in her own bed. She wore her sock monkey pajamas (so much nicer to see than that damn hospital gown) and had wasted no time surrounding herself with her favorite stuffed animals, most of which Eliot had given her. She'd propped herself up on her pillows, and declaring that she wasn't sleepy, began setting up a game of Exploding Kittens on her bed.

"Mom says I can have whatever I want for dinner, so I'm trying to decide between ice cream and cereal."

"Why not both?" Eliot encouraged her, ignoring her sister's glare. Audrey's eyes almost doubled in size as she considered this nutritionally devoid option. "Before you make up your mind, I have something for you." She pulled the Segatti's bakery box from her bag and handed it over, enjoying the look of pure delight on Audrey's face as she peeked inside. She extracted a chocolate glazed donut from the box and immediately sank her teeth into it.

"What do you think? Totally worth leaving the hospital, right?"

Audrey giggled and nodded vigorously. "It might even be worth going back," she said after she swallowed, which merited another glare from her mother.

"Or I could just bring you more because you like them, and you could avoid the hospital entirely."

"I like that plan better," Georgie said before she stole a piece of her daughter's treat and moaned her appreciation.

"Me too," Audrey chimed in.

"Then it's decided. Audrey's job is to stay out of the hospital, and I'll work on wrangling more of these from the magical woman who makes them."

"Tell us about this woman. She sounds special."

From the look on her sister's face, she had a preconceived and erroneous notion about the donut maker. Eliot almost hated to contradict her. "She's blond."

"And how do you feel about that?"

"Better her than me. Dark hair really sells my whole look, you know?"

"Don't be obtuse. You know what I'm asking."

"I do, but you're asking about the wrong woman. The donut maker is the best friend."

"What are you guys talking about?" Audrey had grabbed a second treat while her mother and aunt were distracted with Eliot's stalled love life.

"I thought we were talking about the woman your Zizi is in love with, but apparently there are many new women in her life."

"Too many," she sighed, the memory of Emilia's earlier revelation sinking in. She supposed it was nice to have an explanation for Harper's hasty departure—at least she knew it wasn't her. It was some other "her" causing the trouble, and even though she didn't know this woman or Harper's history with her, she couldn't help but question the strength of their relationship if Harper was going out to dinners and bars without her. Not to mention her expert flirting. What kind of girlfriend could this woman be if Harper felt so unencumbered by their alleged commitment?

"How come you aren't smiling anymore, Zizi?"

"I'm just feeling bad about something I did, but I promise to be all better by your birthday." She had no idea if she could keep that promise.

"You can be sad if that's how you're feeling. You don't need to pretend."

She pulled her niece into an embrace. What a sweet, wonderful kid to care so much about how she was feeling when Audrey really just needed to focus on her own well-being. She kissed her pale forehead and held on to her longer than usual.

"Thanks for that, little one. I'll promise to try to feel better. How does that sound?"

"Seems fair."

"Now, is there anything special you want me to bring?"

"Other than donuts?"

"Or one of these special new women in your life?"

"Don't tell your grandmother," she pointedly ignored Georgie's suggestion, "but the lady who makes those donuts is also making your birthday cake."

"Is it going to be a donut?"

"How about some donuts on the side? And if they aren't available on Saturday, I'll just have to keep going back until she has more." The combination of Audrey's grin and a legitimate excuse to visit the bakery (probably when Harper was likely to be there), brought her own smile back. And it didn't even fade at her sister's laser-like focus on her that brought with it the promise of a future interrogation.

Harper spotted her mother across the restaurant, sitting in a booth sipping her iced tea, unaware that she was about to hijack their weekly lunch with Big Personal Questions. She almost felt bad about disrupting her mother's serenity with her romantic drama, but Em was right (again) that she needed help figuring things out.

She'd spent the remainder of last night pondering the situation. Not by choice, but because her brain wouldn't give her a break from the questions that her friend (and her own behavior) had raised. She successfully tabled the "What do I want?" question for a few hours—long enough to wrangle with her perplexing omission of Caroline from her every conversation with Eliot. She tried to come up with an explanation that made sense—the timing wasn't right, or she and Eliot were more or less business associates, so it would be inappropriate to talk about her personal life—anything other than the suggestion that she liked Eliot. But no matter how imaginative she got, she knew the simplest explanation was also the one that made the most sense. She liked Eliot. But somehow admitting that didn't magically make all her other problems go away. She still didn't know what to do about that or if she should even be considering doing anything about it; hence her impending derailment of her normally lighthearted and fun lunchtime with her mom.

Her stomach was in knots and she felt shaky, like every muscle in her body had atrophied. She wasn't sure she was ready to welcome her mom's input on her love life, but she needed to do something other than replay Em's commentary and worry that she'd ruined her relationship with Caroline and her chances with Eliot. Yes, she was aware that the fact that she had both of those concerns at the same time more or less answered her questions, but she wasn't up to facing logic.

Once she told her mother, though, she would have to do more than brood, and she was both terrified and eager to hear her input. Lucy Maxfield's word wasn't necessarily gospel, but it was close. Harper knew that even though her mom didn't care for Caroline, she wouldn't let her opinion of the person cloud her judgment on the matter, which was another reason she was nervous about this conversation. If her mom genuinely believed she'd be better off ending things with Caroline and going out with Eliot, she honestly didn't know what she would do with that guidance. Would she follow her mother's advice, advice she had sought, even if she didn't know herself if that was what she really wanted? Or would she run from it and allow her life to continue as it had for the past year?

"I need to ask you about my love life," she blurted once the waitress took their orders and disappeared in the direction of the kitchen.

"Well, that's a big topic for a Thursday afternoon. Did something happen?"

"Maybe," she said and grabbed a package of saltines from the ubiquitous basket of free restaurant carbs. She inspected the crackers carefully as she offered the CliffsNotes version of her current romantic dilemma.

"Do you like this Eliot?" Her mother's voice remained neutral, but she didn't dare meet her eyes for fear of seeing any answer other than the one she wanted written there.

"Em thinks I do."

Her soft hand reached across the table and covered hers, eliminating the cracker distraction and forcing her to look up. "And what do you think?"

"I think, maybe I do." She felt tears forming and was mortified to be crying in a booth by the window of a crowded downtown restaurant. It didn't matter that the people around them were too busy with their own messed up lives to notice hers.

"I think maybe you do too." Their tender moment was cut short by the arrival of their food and their waitress's brusque inquiry about condiments, which they declined.

"So, what?" she asked when they were alone again. "I just say screw this commitment I've made because someone new caught my eye? I tell Caroline, 'Thanks for the good time, but I'm on to something new'?"

"I didn't say that, but since you brought it up—"

"You want me to dump her."

"I would never tell you who to date. You know that." She did know that. Her mother had never once meddled in her love life or said a negative word about anyone she'd dated, whether they deserved it or not. "I'm not telling you what to do or who to choose. But I have to ask, why are you so committed to salvaging your relationship with Caroline?"

"We've been together for a year. That's the longest relationship I've ever had. Why would I just walk away from that?"

"If longevity is the only reason you want to stay—"

"It's not. I love her."

"Or maybe you love what she represents." Her voice was firm but gentle, and the sympathetic look in her eye was almost unbearable.

"And what is that?"

She was sure she wanted to hear this answer about as much as she wanted a gravel enema, but she couldn't leave the conversation incomplete. She'd already heard too much that she hadn't wanted to. How much worse could more painful revelations be?

"What you've been looking for ever since your brother died, a hero." She'd been pushing her food around the plate more than eating it, but now she pushed it aside, her appetite completely gone. "Don't get mad at me. You asked for my opinion."

"That was before I knew what that would feel like."

"Have you never noticed what all of your girlfriends have had in common?"

"They're all women?"

Her mother favored her with her most long-suffering smile, the one that always made her feel stupid, like she'd missed something obvious.

"First there was Christy, the captain of the basketball team. Now, I don't generally think of athletes as being particularly heroic, but she certainly fit the bill, especially when she joined the army after high school. Obviously, that wasn't great for your relationship, but I don't think it diminished her appeal in the slightest."

"I didn't date Christy."

"No, you didn't tell me you were dating Christy, but I have eyes. I saw what was happening. And even if all of your late night 'study sessions' weren't a dead giveaway, your prom dates were. If the four of you hadn't been using each other as mutual beards, I would've been shocked."

She shouldn't have been surprised that her mother hadn't been fooled by her near total incompetence at subterfuge. Her mom was too perceptive and loving not to be aware of what was really going on, especially since all they had was each other.

"And then you met Theresa, the lifeguard. I will admit she was good-looking, but that's about all she had going for her, unless you're someone with a hero complex. She wasn't terribly kind or bright, but she looked good in a swimsuit."

"Mom!"

"As if you weren't thinking the same thing the entire three months she held your attention." Harper squirmed in her chair. This conversation was turning out to be all kinds of fun. "After her came the EMT, I don't remember her name, and I'd be surprised if you did. She didn't even last as long as Theresa. But then you found a cop, a firefighter and a brief rekindling of your non-relationship with Christy when she was home on leave. All of it was very exciting, and they all have two things in common."

"Other than failing to impress my mother, what's that?"

"All of them attracted you because of what they did, not who they were, and none of them managed to hold your attention for long because of it."

"But Caroline has held my attention. We've been together for a year, remember?"

"You started dating a year ago, but in that year, how much time do you think you've really been together?"

She actually started doing the math in her head before realizing that even the need for such calculations proved her mother's point.

"How have I never noticed this about myself?"

"You were too busy having fun to think about it."

"That paints a charming portrait of me."

"I'd say it's a more common picture than most of us would care to admit."

"So what do I do now?"

"Oh, honey, I can't answer that for you." She offered a gentle smile and took her hand. "Blake's death left such a big scar on your heart. I know you tried to help him and that you blamed yourself for a long time. Perhaps you still do. But you couldn't have rescued him, sweet girl. It was too late. I hope you know that."

"I do. Now."

"And do you know that you don't need to keep chasing after someone who could save him? You don't have to sacrifice your own happiness out of guilt about your brother's death."

"I'm not sacrificing any happiness."

Her mother looked away for a moment before turning her kind eyes back on her. "Just promise to consider what will make you truly happy and don't be afraid to really go after whatever it is you want."

"I promise," she said, wondering if she really would.

CHAPTER THIRTEEN

An unexpected case of nerves washed over Eliot when she spotted Harper through the window of Segatti's Bakery. She didn't know what to expect when she walked through the door. This was their first contact since the kiss, and on the very real possibility that it would also be their last, she allowed herself a moment to admire her before she approached.

Harper seemed impossibly perky for a Saturday morning, and somehow the plain white apron she wore over her pale blue T-shirt looked just as enticing as the other pulse-raising outfits she'd worn. She laughed with the couple at her register—one of those hearty, full-body kind of laughs where her head fell back, exposing her long, entirely kissable throat. She was adorable and charming and completely off-limits, Eliot thought as she entered.

"You took my advice on the cake." Harper's smile was nervous, like she didn't quite know what to expect from this exchange—a standard business transaction or guerrilla kissing tactics.

"I'm really here for the donuts. The cake is just a cover." Eliot didn't know if it was the right strategy, but she opted for a lighter approach to help put Harper at ease.

"I've seen this kind of addiction before. It's a deliciously glazed slippery slope. Are you sure you can handle it?"

"It's already looking dire. You wouldn't happen to have any equally habit-forming coffee back there, would you?"

"You're hard core. And you're in luck. Em has the best coffee in the city."

Eliot gratefully accepted a cup from Harper and paused to savor the tantalizing aroma. She took a sip and had to stop herself from moaning. "Is there anything she can't do?"

"Make an honest woman out of you." Harper's face instantly turned the most magnificent shade of red after she uttered the words.

"There are so many ways I could take that, and not one of them makes sense. Care to fill me in?"

Emilia approached the counter, large cake box in her hands, glower firmly in place. "She's been trying to set us up."

"I might be even more confused now. Why would Harper think you need help getting a date?" Eliot asked.

"Right back at you."

"Which is why I thought you'd be perfect for each other," Harper grumbled and blushed again.

"Guess I ruined that plan," Eliot said.

"Which I've been meaning to thank you for."

"It was my pleasure." Eliot shrugged and looked to Harper. "Do you have a minute to talk?"

"I'm at work."

"I know, and I promise not to take up too much of your time."

Emilia nudged her friend away from the register. "Go ahead. I can handle things up here for a little while."

"I'm sorry. I know this isn't the best time, but I wanted to apologize again. If I had known, I wouldn't have—"

"I know. I should have told you about her, about Caroline. I'm sorry I put you in an awkward position."

"Don't try to take credit for my mistake."

"I was just—"

"Blaming yourself for not prefacing all of your encounters with a disclaimer that you're not single?" She shrugged adorably, a more genuine smile appearing. "You should let me make it up to you."

"What do you have in mind?"

"I hadn't thought that far in advance." Eliot winked and kicked herself for her habitual flirting. "How about I start by helping you with the fundraiser?"

"You're already helping with the fundraiser."

"I want to do more. It's coming up fast, and you probably have a million things to do."

"If I ever get a chance to stop and count, I'll let you know."

"So let me ease that burden a little," Eliot offered.

"Really?"

"Of course. We can start on Monday if you're free."

"That means a lot to me. I thought I'd run you off."

"Technically, you were the one who ran off."

"I guess we've entered the joking phase of your apology."

Just then an elderly gentleman entered the store, offering an expansive, effusive greeting to all. He plucked his cap from his head, folded it into the pocket of his jacket and without hesitating, rushed to the spot where she and Harper stood waiting to resume the conversation he'd brought to an abrupt halt.

"Hello, miss." He clutched Eliot's hand in both of his and held on like a lifeline. "You must be the girlfriend I've heard so much about. It's a pleasure to meet you. I can see why Harper speaks so highly of you. She's a looker," he mock whispered to an increasingly red-faced Harper. "I'll leave you lovebirds to talk. It looks like Emilia has my order ready."

"I'm so sorry about that."

"I don't know why you should be," Eliot said. "He had nothing but nice things to say about me."

"He's such a sweet man. I didn't want to embarrass him."

"I'm really not offended that he thinks we make a good couple."

"Yeah, well." Harper looked everywhere but at her. She couldn't help reveling in the effect of this friendly older fellow's unsuspecting vote for Team Eliot.

"He never would have said all that if you'd told him you aren't my girlfriend."

"You could have said the same thing, though I know it can be challenging for you to share information about her. On the other hand, he actually knew she existed." Harper's expression was pure frustration, but she made no attempt to defend herself. "Apparently, I'm a looker."

"He has cataracts."

"A condition known for enhancing the beauty of strangers."

"Don't you have a birthday party to go to?"

"And some new fundraising responsibilities to prep for. See you Monday." That time she savored every second of the wink that brought another astounding blush to Harper's gorgeous face.

"That seemed to go well." Em was smirking. Harper hated when she smirked because it was usually the precursor to gloating.

"I wouldn't designate it a success just yet, but I suppose it could have been much worse."

"Tell me this. Do you really think you can avoid temptation by working so closely with her? Isn't that what got you into trouble in the first place?"

"No. A lack of communication got us into trouble, but now we know everything we need to know about each other. I don't see why there should be any problems."

"That's a lot of unsupervised proximity."

"I think we can survive a few hours without a chaperone, but if you're volunteering to pitch in and keep us on our best behavior, I can find plenty for you to do."

"I would make a terrible chaperone. I'm trying to encourage this behavior."

"A simple, 'No, thank you. I'm busy,' would have sufficed."

"No thank you. I'm busy." She smirked again. "I hope your girlfriend will be all right with this, assuming you plan to tell her you've recruited a new helper."

"Since I'm not telling her everything about our relationship, per your advice, I think she'll be fine with it. Why would she object to me being less stressed out?"

"Because, as usual, she'll be thinking of how this will affect her, not how it will benefit you. As soon as you mention that your helper is a woman, she's going to have questions. I'd bet on it."

"She's allowed to show an interest in my life. Isn't that what you complain she doesn't do enough of?"

"Except she'll be doing it to protect her interests, not because she genuinely cares about what you're doing or how it affects you."

"Because she's completely evil, I know."

"Not completely. Just mostly."

"What a warm sentiment. You two will be BFFs before long."

"I can take it back, you know. I'm more than happy about hanging on to my seething hatred for the woman, but since you asked me to try to get along with her, that's what I'm doing."

"When she's not around?"

"Gotta start somewhere. But for the record, Eliot doesn't have any trouble getting along with your best friend."

"Maybe my best friend should take advantage of that."

"Stop right there."

"So you can play matchmaker but I can't?"

"The difference is that Eliot and I make good friends while Eliot and you make a good couple."

"I'm done having this conversation with you. Go frost something."

"Your evasiveness is adorable and pointless. Mark my words, this is happening. Even Mr. Sutcliffe agrees."

"He's a sweet man, not a psychic."

"Maybe he's both."

"Maybe you need to start looking for a new best friend."

CHAPTER FOURTEEN

"Hey, Mom." Eliot breezed into her sister's kitchen, balancing her bakery haul in one hand and her present for Audrey in the other. Still in a good mood, she leaned in to kiss her mother's cheek. "Where's Jimmy?"

"I sent your father to the store for ice."

"Stepfather," she corrected and watched her mother's face fall. "It's fifty degrees outside. How much ice do we need?"

"Probably not much, but I needed to give him something to do before I killed him for trying to be helpful." She had all four burners going, and the whole house smelled amazing, like the Sundays of her childhood. Then, too, she would send Jimmy on some needless errand, leaving her to cook in peace.

Eliot liberated the cake from its telltale bakery box and placed it on the counter, noting the barest pause in the otherwise ricochet chopping that filled the air. Cautiously optimistic, she snagged a slice of green pepper from the cutting board and waited for the inevitable reprimand, but her mother just resumed chopping without a word. She looked tired, more than could be excused by the pressures of cooking for a seven-year-old's birthday party, and Eliot felt a sudden, alarming worry for her well-being. Despite the challenges of their relationship, the thought of her mother succumbing to some debilitating illness was terrifying.

"What are you frowning about? You should smile more. You're so pretty when you do."

"Thanks, Mom. That's what every girl longs to hear. She's unattractive unless she's smiling."

"You know that's not what I meant. You're a beautiful young woman. Even with all that junk on your arms."

Now she did smile. "I hope you realize every time you criticize my tattoos, you inspire me to get another one."

"Where could you possibly put any more?"

"Maybe there's a face tattoo in my future." She smiled innocently.

"Eliot Anne DeSanto, don't you even joke about such things."

She gave her mother one more affectionate kiss on the cheek and then placed one of Audrey's donuts on a plate. As she weighed the candle versus no-candle decision, her mother interrupted.

"You brought donuts? Why would you bring breakfast? It's one in the afternoon, and I'm making a million pounds of pasta for eight people."

"I don't think I want to live in a world where afternoon donut consumption is frowned upon."

"I don't even know how to talk to you sometimes."

"That I can believe," she called over her shoulder as she went in search of a more appreciative audience for her pastry offerings.

Somewhere between cleaning up after lunch and opening presents, which Audrey insisted on doing before cake so that one didn't distract her from the other, she pulled Georgie to the side.

"I'm kind of in the middle of throwing a party here. If you're not on fire or missing a limb, you will be soon."

"I'll be quick. I promise." She flicked her gaze in the direction of Georgie's not very pregnant-looking belly. "I wanted to check in with you about your development. Have you talked to any doctors yet?"

"No. In part because I've been busy planning this party you're currently interrupting with your poorly timed consideration."

"What else is holding you back?"

"Fear mostly. But also taking care of Audrey."

"That fear might go away if you talk to her doctors the next time you see them."

"Or it might multiply."

"I'll go with you if you want. I'll even ask for you."

"I think I'll be okay, but thank you for the offer. Was there anything else? Or can I get back to my house full of people?"

"Remember the kiss?"

"I assume you mean the one that didn't end well."

"That's the one."

"Do you have information?"

"She has a girlfriend. That's why she ran away."

"Why are you kissing someone who's in a relationship?"

"Because I want to give our mother one more thing to be proud of me for. Obviously, I didn't know about the girlfriend."

"How serious is it?"

"If it's serious enough to earn her the label of girlfriend, it's too serious for me to consider future kissing."

"You're still thinking about it, aren't you?"

"All the time," she whined as her sister pushed her back toward the festivities.

After unwrapping each gift and carefully reading the card attached, Audrey walked over to whoever was responsible and gave them a hearty hug. It slowed the process considerably, but it was a sweet reminder of how lucky they were to have this little girl.

When her gift was the last unopened one left on the table, Eliot wished she could slow time so she could enjoy the moment even more. For her part, Audrey facilitated that desire by carefully peeling the tape off the paper, so as not to damage the hodgepodge assortment of animals that Zizi had drawn on the otherwise plain brown paper. As soon as she saw what was inside, she gasped, and her eyes grew wide. For several moments, she alternated between hugging the frame to her tiny body and holding it out before her to stare at and smile.

"Thank you, Zizi," she whispered into Eliot's ear as she hugged her, her bony arms holding her tight. "I love it."

"I love you." The only thing preventing Eliot from squeezing her tighter was the fear of hurting her frail little body.

She had set the picture on the table to issue her thanks, and the other guests had taken the opportunity to see what she had received. Most of the people there—Georgie, Vinnie, his parents and brother—all expressed amazed appreciation. It was nice to hear, but it paled in comparison to Audrey's reaction. Still, she allowed herself to bask in the praise a little, until her mother brought that to an abrupt end.

"It's not very practical."

"Well, I was going to get her a printing calculator and a columnar pad, but then I remembered she's seven, not an accountant. Once she turns eight, though, look out. It's all orthopedic shoes and day planners."

"Or maybe a nice doll or a sweater."

A million responses flooded her mind, but instead of getting into a fight with her mother and ruining her niece's birthday party, she excused herself from the room.

Needing some kind of release, she took her aggressions out on the collection of plates and glasses crowding the countertop. The sink hardly had more than half an inch of water and a smattering of bubbles before Georgie's arms were around her.

"It's the perfect gift."

"You've always been a little impractical."

"It's my downfall. Mom's is—"

"Me?"

"It might be a little more complicated than that."

"Feels pretty straightforward to me."

Georgie pulled her away from the sink and sat her down at the kitchen table. "I've watched the two of you sparring my entire life, and I've paid attention."

"You need a better hobby."

Though she hated to admit it, she wanted, just once, for her mother to be proud of her. Or at least not ashamed. Nothing Georgie did fazed Carla DeSanto, not even getting pregnant outside of marriage and refusing to marry the father of her child for five years. But if Eliot picked at a hangnail or cleared her throat, there'd be hell to pay. She didn't get it and doubted she ever would.

"I'm not sure that it has anything to do with either of us."

Georgie's comment brought Eliot back to her most recent failure. "If Mom's eternal disappointment in me and never-ending pride in you has nothing to do with me or you, I'm even more confused."

"Honestly, I think it's more about our fathers than us, or at least your father." She shrugged, as if she had been asked whether she wanted fries or mashed potatoes as a side instead of lobbing a mental and emotional curveball at her sister.

"You're telling me my whole life has been a letdown because she regrets sleeping with my dad?"

"Pretty much." Again with the shrug, and as much as she wanted to slap her for her nonchalance, her theory made some sense.

"She's the one who slept with him. Why do I get punished for it?" She returned her attention to the dishes.

"I know it's not fair, El, but she can't exactly take it out on the person she's really mad at, so all her disappointment in the man whose name you share gets dumped onto you."

"How am I ever supposed to overcome that? I'm never going to have a decent relationship with her, am I?" Surprisingly, she felt tears threaten. No matter how much she thought she'd moved past her anger and frustration, the subject of her mother always found a way to get to her.

"You could try talking to her."

"I talk to her all the time."

"No, you argue with her and push her buttons. You flex your sarcasm muscles, but you don't talk."

"I'll put it on my list."

"It's appreciated."

"If you promise to talk to the doctors."

"Fine."

"Are you girls ever coming back?" Their mother called out before she entered the room. "We can't cut the cake without you, and we need to find out if it tastes as good as it looks."

"Did she just compliment me?"

"Close enough." They fell in line behind her as they made their way back to the dining room.

"We can always eat the cake I brought. Just in case."

She turned to look at Georgie, long-suffering expression firmly in place. "You owe me twenty bucks."

"I recruited some more help today," Harper announced.

"That's nice." Caroline folded her blouse precisely and laid it on the chair beside Harper's bed. She didn't turn around to gauge her excitement over this development. Instead, she simply moved on to the next phase of her meticulous disrobing.

"It is nice. Though I suppose, technically, I didn't do any recruiting. My volunteer sought me out to volunteer for me."

"I'm glad you've got help." There went the pants, perfectly creased and placed atop their well-coordinated top. She sat on the edge of the bed—still not bothering to look at the woman she was undressing for—and removed her socks, first the left, then the right, before folding them and adding them to the stack.

"Me too." She tugged at the hem of her shirt but let it go rather than lifting it over her head. "Especially since Eliot didn't know anything about the cause before we met."

"You scored another convert. Good for you." She slipped out of her bra and didn't seem to notice that Harper was not only still fully dressed, but also not scrambling to get her naked. She was, in fact, as interested in having sex with Caroline as Caroline was in her news.

"Yeah. Good for me."

Caroline scooted toward the head of the bed and after brief eye contact, began kissing her neck. Her hands moved to Harper's jeans, and as she worked to unbutton them, Harper's hand stilled hers.

"Is something wrong?"

"Why don't you care about this?"

"I care about this very much." She kissed her again and laid her hand on her crotch.

"Not sex." She swatted her hand away. "Why don't you care about what I'm telling you?"

"Didn't I say I was happy for you?"

"You did, but you couldn't be bothered to ask me any questions about her."

"Her? What her?"

"My new volunteer."

"You said his name was Eliot."

"At least you heard something I said."

She sat up and folded her hands in her lap. "So tell me more about this volunteer of yours. Who is this woman? A retiree with lots of free time?"

"Hardly. You're closer to retirement than she is." She instantly regretted that.

"What the hell is that supposed to mean? I thought you said it didn't bother you that I'm older than you."

"It doesn't bother me. You know that. It's just a little odd to think that someone must be retired in order to volunteer her time, especially considering who you've been sleeping with for the past year."

"So she's younger than me. Is she pretty?"

"That's what you're interested in knowing? Not if she brings any special skills to the cause or what might have inspired her to give up her time? And she has almost no free time, by the way. She has two jobs, and her family takes up a lot of her time."

"She sounds like a real find."

"Don't be such a snob. What's so wrong with someone working hard and caring about her family?"

"Nothing. I wasn't judging her. I don't even know her."

"No, you don't, but you could. You could help with the fundraiser too, and then you could get to know her." Harper had no idea why she'd just suggested that. Really, the last thing she wanted was for Caroline and Eliot to spend any time together. The farther apart they stayed, the better off her life would be.

"You know I would if I could."

Apparently she needn't have worried. Unlike Eliot, Caroline had no plans to devote any of her time or energy to her girlfriend's cause. And, just as Em had predicted, she seemed more concerned with Eliot as competition than happy that she had more help. It was disheartening, but she supposed she shouldn't have been all that surprised. In all their time together, Caroline had shown the smallest amount of interest possible in Allies and her work with them.

The only time they'd spent more than five minutes discussing the organization was when Caroline dissuaded Harper from taking a low-paying, entry-level position with them, a position that could have led Harper where she wanted to be with the group. But Caroline had convinced her that she'd be better off working for an established firm, making good money, paying off her student loans so that she'd be in a better position to contribute to the group financially if she wanted. Though she'd been ready to cut all the corners so that she could work her way toward her dream job, she'd let herself be convinced that getting work experience and a decent paycheck would be worthwhile in the end. She hadn't fully believed Caroline, but she also hadn't wanted to keep fighting. And now she was trapped in her job, wishing she had never listened to her.

But she couldn't blame her, not entirely. Though Caroline had pushed relentlessly and argued her case effectively, the decision to abandon her dream had been Harper's alone. And now she had to take direction from someone who knew less about the organization and the role she'd filled than she did. It was infuriating and humiliating, and she realized bitterly, something she could have avoided entirely if she were more like Eliot. Not only would she never have allowed herself to be talked out of her dream, but she also wouldn't have agreed to work in hell with a smarmy sexist. She wouldn't have traded her integrity for a steady paycheck.

If another position opened up, she swore she would go for it, stability be damned. She'd work extra shifts at the bakery to make ends meet if she had to or learn to tend bar like Eliot, but she wasn't going to spend the next forty years smiling politely at the Dougs of the world. And she wasn't going to let Caroline off so easily this time.

"You could do a little."

"When would I do that? Would you like me to spend time working for your cause instead of being with you?"

"You could do both at the same time. That's what Eliot's doing."

That got her attention. "How much time is she going to be spending with you?"

"I'm not sure yet. We're meeting on Monday so I can train her. She's also my artist for the fundraiser, so we'll have to spend time finalizing the details of that. And, of course, she'll be at the fundraiser."

"Where are you meeting?"

"We haven't discussed it yet, but we'll probably do it here."

"Shouldn't you go somewhere more public?"

"Shouldn't you trust your girlfriend?" A twinge of guilt accompanied that comment.

"I just think you'd get more done at the library."

"Where we can't make phone calls?"

"What about a coffee shop?"

"It's too noisy. Also, I have everything I need right here, and I'd have to schlep it all to work and then to a coffee shop. Life would just be easier if we could work here."

"Is this really how professionals do this sort of thing?"

"Well, I'm not a professional, am I? Maybe if I hadn't taken your career advice, I would have an office to work out of instead of using my kitchen table."

"Don't get so upset. I'm just concerned about you."

"Really? Because it seems like you're concerned about yourself."

"I want this to work out for you. I'm so proud of the work you've done, the work you're doing, and I don't want you to compromise the quality for anything."

"Even if that means working closely with another woman?"

"How closely are we talking?"

"We'll probably sit at the same table. We might have dinner while we work, and Em will probably join us. It promises to be quite a sexy evening of securing donors and vendors and proofing ads. I may swoon just thinking about it."

"You're so cute when you're sarcastic."

"Don't be condescending. You're already in trouble."

"I'm sorry if I upset you. I didn't mean to."

"I just wish you cared about my work as much as I care about yours. I know it's not quite on the same level, but I am saving lives. What I do with Allies makes a difference. It would be nice if you cared."

"I do care."

"Just not enough to help me."

"Sweetheart, if I could, I would devote all of my time to you and help you so much you'd be sick of me. But I have other responsibilities. I can't turn my back on them just because I love you."

"Maybe you could try a little harder to show that?"

"Can I start now?" She kissed her without waiting for an answer, and even though her body responded as hungrily as it usually did, her mind wasn't completely on board. She couldn't turn off the part of her brain that insisted there was something wrong. It replayed Em's criticism of Caroline—how she focused on her own needs over Harper's, how their arguments and sexual reconciliations were so common that they characterized the entirety of their relationship. And then her mother crept in with her comments about staying with Caroline because of what she represented rather than who she was. And who she was didn't quite measure up to someone who was generous, thoughtful and compassionate. Someone like Eliot.

And just like that, the woman she wasn't supposed to be thinking about at all, certainly not now, took center stage in her thoughts and wouldn't let go. What would Emilia make of this development? As she closed her eyes, she imagined Eliot's blue eyes focused on her.

CHAPTER FIFTEEN

"You know you're asking for trouble, right?"

Harper had expected her announcement that Eliot would be coming to their apartment to be met with mild irritation or grudging acceptance. Smug chastising was something of a surprise. "Unless monumental flirting is on your to-do list, you're not going to get anything accomplished," Em said.

"But we'll have you to keep us on our best behavior."

"I'm not a warden. Or a miracle worker. And, in case I haven't made this clear, I'm not exactly opposed to you dating Eliot. I just want you to break up with Caroline first. You didn't happen to squeeze that in today, did you?"

"I'm not breaking up with Caroline."

"Yet."

"Just because someone attractive comes along doesn't mean I'm going to throw away the past year of my life."

"Fine. You're a loyal and trustworthy girlfriend whose habitual flirting with another woman led to kissing. Kissing that you enjoyed. But by all means, let a long-standing mistake be the reason you don't find real happiness."

"Are you finished?"

"No, but I'll save the rest for later."

"Something to look forward to." She checked the clock and realized that Eliot was due any minute. "I have to change before she gets here."

"Why don't you just wait until she arrives to slip into something more comfortable?"

"Isn't that the sort of behavior you were warning me about?"

"I'm just trying to rush the inevitable."

"If she shows up, just—"

"Send her to your room?"

Harper scowled, already regretting this decision.

"I'm only trying to help," Emilia insisted.

"Don't try so hard."

She would be lying if she said she hadn't had some of the same reservations as Emilia. Worse, she'd dismissed them on the completely nonexistent strength of her resolve. She didn't think Eliot would try kissing her again, but she also didn't think she'd have the willpower to end it so quickly if she did.

She considered the contents of her closet, dismissing most of her clothes outright. Normally after work she threw on her loungiest loungewear, but tonight that wouldn't do. She heard the buzzer as she pulled her most flattering pair of jeans over her hips and felt a momentary panic. She didn't have time to deliberate over a top, but she also couldn't just grab anything. Not that Eliot was a stickler for dress codes—half the time she'd seen her, she'd been in jeans and a tank top, hardly the uniform of the fashion police. Still, Harper felt paralyzed by indecision.

Em's and Eliot's muted voices carried to her room, urging her to action. She grabbed a light sweater, and convinced she looked good enough to face her helper, opened the door to whatever the night was about to bring.

Though it was a work session—very much not a date—Eliot still brought a bottle of wine with her. A little wine couldn't hurt. It might even help, depending on what they were doing that evening. She honestly didn't know what she was in for. Phone calls? Envelope stuffing? Physical labor? She had no idea what to expect (other than a disappointing lack of kissing). But she'd promised to help, so she was determined to see this through.

Not that she hadn't frequently considered bailing, especially since enduring more than one anti-pep talk from her self-appointed romance cheering squad. Both Georgie and Alice had checked in during the day, and both had left her with the alarming concern that, given the scarcity of her philanthropic activities, not only would she be in completely foreign territory (in the middle of painfully platonic seas), but she might also come face-to-face with the woman she'd unintentionally cuckolded.

Initially she'd been buoyant at Harper's suggestion that they work at the apartment she shared with Emilia. She knew better than to read too much into a proposal that had surely sprung more from convenience than a radical change of heart and relationship status, but she couldn't help the happy jolt that accompanied the thought of spending time with Harper in such a cozy setting. But then her sister and best friend had to destroy her unfounded joy with the entirely unwelcome possibility that her evening would include a healthy dose of collegiality with the woman whose existence had ruined everything.

She wasn't sure she could handle watching Harper be in love with someone else. Not that she expected them to be making out or cuddling. It hardly seemed likely that there would be any romantic overtures while they were trying to save the world. Still, just knowing that after she left, the romance would surely commence had her considering coming down with an imaginary illness. Tempting as it was to avoid the painful awkwardness of quality time with the woman who stood between her and happiness with Harper, she wouldn't back out now. She'd made a commitment, and she intended to honor it. And who knew? Maybe meeting the girlfriend would make it easier somehow. Maybe she was an amazing human, the kind of person Harper deserved to be with. That wouldn't make her situation any better, but it would be nice for Harper.

Emilia, not the woman she'd been looking forward to seeing, welcomed her inside, further dashing her willful optimism about the evening. And though she saw no signs of the girlfriend anywhere in the spacious apartment, she also saw no signs of the woman who'd been plaguing her thoughts for most of the day. She was about to check her phone for a last-minute cancellation text when Emilia grabbed the wine she'd forgotten she was holding.

"Someone has the right idea about charity work." She wandered off toward the kitchen, leaving Eliot to make herself comfortable. "Harper should be out in a minute. She had to change out of her work clothes."

As her remote hostess talked, she ventured farther into the apartment, noting the overcrowded bookshelves and the homey appeal of the well-used furniture. Aside from some photographs here and there, the space lacked for art—a flaw she immediately decided she had to rectify. If there was one thing she had a surplus of, it was art. She wasn't sure they'd want to decorate their home in comic book drawings, but a sketch or two might be welcome.

"This is going to earn you major points," Emilia called from the kitchen. "When Harp got home, she looked like she either needed to drink or murder someone."

"So, I'm saving lives."

"You're a true American hero." She brought three glasses back with her, and with all signs pointing to a girlfriend-free night, Eliot relaxed and joined her on the couch.

"You brought wine?"

Her head snapped in the direction of Harper's voice. She looked comfortably casual in jeans and a loose-fitting light blue top. Her hair was up in a ponytail, emphasizing the sharp lines of her face and showing off her long, graceful neck.

Their eyes locked, and Eliot's lips parted before the corners turned up into a smile. "Hi."

"Hi." She tucked a loose strand of hair behind her ear and looked around the room nervously.

"Oh, yeah, nothing to worry about here," Emilia muttered as she wandered into the kitchen.

It was weird at first. And so incredibly frustrating. Not just because Harper had to explain everything to Eliot, whose volunteer résumé started and ended with this evening's activities. She was eager to help and happy to take on any of the tasks Harper assigned her, but the lengthy instruction that preceded each undertaking initially made her as much a hindrance as a help.

And then there were the cats. She loved Mary Berry and Avagato, but at this moment she wished they found hiding under the bed half as interesting as the activities currently taking place in their living room. It was mildly challenging to accomplish much with the assistance of two feline know-it-alls, and though Emilia did her best to herd them, they seemed to instinctively know (and savor) their potential for being nuisances and thus invariably selected the worst possible location to acrobatically lick their hindquarters. As soon as Emilia removed one from the middle of the activity, the other would take its place, like an adorably aggravating mythological creature.

To her credit, Eliot took their help in stride. She didn't seem the least bit fazed when Avagato settled himself on the contract she'd been proofing. She simply shifted her attention to the phone calls that needed to be made. And when he caught on that his ploy for attention had failed, he moved over to her new project, freeing up the promotional flyer she'd been tweaking before he made his appearance. It was an impressive dance of feline needs and human adaptability. Harper had lucked out. After close to thirty minutes of restlessness, Mary Berry curled up in her lap and fell into a deep slumber. While it impacted her ability to do anything that involved moving from her seat, she had no trouble making calls and answering emails.

They'd finally settled into a more or less productive flow, the companionable near-silence that had settled over them lasting several minutes before curiosity got the better of her.

"Why did you offer to do this? Really."

"You needed help. I thought I could be useful. That's really all there was to it. I promise I don't have a hidden agenda."

"So you aren't thinking about what happened?"

"Are you?"

"Of course not," she lied.

"Okay."

"That's it? Just 'okay' and you're satisfied?"

"I'm far from satisfied where you're concerned." Their eyes locked, and her voice settled into a low register that could only be called sexy. "I suspect it would take years, possibly the rest of my life and yours for me to be satisfied with you."

Harper felt the immense weight of her eyelids as she blinked. She licked her lips, swallowed hard and felt herself drifting toward Eliot.

"But you have a girlfriend, so you should probably let me know if us working together will be a problem," Eliot said.

"No problem at all."

She cleared her throat and considered excusing herself to splash water on her face and find some way to deal with her suddenly damp panties. If this was Eliot on her "just friends" setting, she would need to find a litany of libido-dampening thoughts to combat the seductiveness that practically pulsated from her. She supposed she could try to focus on her girlfriend, the reason she resisted her attraction to the woman who now had four thousand percent of her attention, but at this moment she was having a hard time remembering her own name, let alone her girlfriend.

The sound of the buzzer startled her out of her thoughts and sent both cats scurrying from the certain apocalypse at the door. She wasn't expecting anyone else and felt a volatile blend of surprise and irritation when she heard Caroline's tinny voice through the intercom asking if she could come up.

CHAPTER SIXTEEN

The formerly playful atmosphere Eliot had been enjoying disappeared with the arrival of the newcomer and the dense fog of discomfort she ushered in with her. While Emilia's disposition slid from easygoing mirth to unfettered hostility, Harper's previously mellow mood was suddenly laced with tension. Eliot didn't know why they both seemed so aggrieved, but the uneasiness affected her as well, especially when Harper abruptly ended the hearty (if not entirely welcome) kiss she'd been greeted with and there stood Audrey's oncologist, Dr. West. She immediately laid claim to Harper with a possessive arm around the waist, and Eliot resisted the urge to clean her glasses as if to wipe this image from her sight.

For her part, Harper didn't seem as happy to see her visitor as Eliot would have expected. Unless women were just naturally prone to kissing her, this was the mysterious and long-absent girlfriend, and by all appearances her presence was neither expected nor fully appreciated. Harper didn't say as much in words, but her body language spoke volumes. Perhaps it had to do with Eliot. She didn't know if news of their kiss had reached Dr. West, but either way, having both Eliot and her in the same place had to add to Harper's discomfort.

Eliot was about to offer to leave. She hadn't wanted to be around the girlfriend when she was just an unidentified obstacle to Harper, and knowing who she was (and what she'd been doing behind Harper's back) hadn't made the prospect any more appealing. But before Eliot could get the words out, her host and charity mentor excused them both and dragged Dr. West off to her bedroom, leaving her and Emilia to speculate on what was happening.

"That may be the first time she's ever not been happy to see her girlfriend."

"That can't be her girlfriend."

"I agree she's totally wrong for Harper—in almost every way possible—but there she is."

She stared at the closed bedroom door, as if that could reassure her that she was seeing things and wasn't about to add unnecessary turmoil to her life. But even though she couldn't will herself to see the pair behind the door any more than she could will the facts to change themselves, she knew she had seen correctly. Which meant she had some unpleasant business to take care of.

"I know that woman."

"I'm so sorry for you."

"It wasn't a bad thing until this moment. She's one of my niece's doctors."

"Of course she is." Emilia already sounded pained by their discussion. Eliot feared this would be the apex of Emilia's emotions once she heard the rest of the story. This was so not what she expected to come out of this night, and it for sure couldn't be the way Harper envisioned her contributions. Her heart broke for her, thinking of the drastic turn her life was going to take, thanks at least in part to her. But she couldn't keep it to herself, no matter the consequences.

"And she has a girlfriend," Eliot announced.

Emilia blinked at her for a moment while she waited for her to catch up. "You aren't talking about Harper, are you?"

"I can't believe I'm about to say this, but I wish I was."

"What are you saying?"

"When Audrey was first in the hospital, I was heading home, and I saw Dr. West in the lobby. I wanted to thank her for taking such great care of my niece since she really is a good doctor."

"So I've heard." Emilia rose abruptly and retrieved the half-empty bottle of wine from the kitchen, topping off both of their glasses. "I sense we'll be needing strength for this conversation."

"But before I made it across the lobby, another woman approached her from the other side. Their greeting was definitely more romantic than platonic. I didn't want to invade her privacy, so I just kept walking. As far as I know, she never saw me."

"I don't suppose this happened a couple of years ago, before she and Harper started dating?"

"More like a couple of weeks ago."

"Son of a bitch. We have to tell Harper."

"*You* have to tell Harper. I can't do it."

"I'm not the one who saw the love of her life making out with another woman."

"And you're also not the one who's interested in dating her. Or whose niece is in the care of the woman you'd be ratting out. I can't put Audrey's health at risk."

"If she's as wonderful a doctor as you people keep claiming, she wouldn't jeopardize her patient's health because she was caught cheating."

"And if it was your niece, would you really take that chance?"

Emilia turned away and shook her head. When she looked back, she had a determined set to her jaw. "I've dreamed about an opportunity like this since they started dating. I thought I would enjoy it more when it came." After two swallows of wine she seemed resolved. "She's not going to believe me. Given my history of Caroline bashing, she's going to assume I'm making things up."

"It's not going to sound any more legitimate coming from the woman who was recently campaigning to get in her pants."

"Is that all she is to you?"

"Not even a little, but given the circumstances, I somehow doubt she'll believe I have noble intentions. And I love that your protective side overrides your already protective side."

"Harper's been through hell, and I will kill you if you hurt her."

"If I ever get the chance to do more than play phone tag with the snow cone vendor for her, I'll take your warning under advisement."

"Good." She nodded once. "So what are we going to do about that situation?" She gestured toward the closed bedroom door with her head.

"I still say you should tell her. She has to know the truth. Even if she won't like it."

"Fine. I'll tell her, but she has blinders on when it comes to Caroline. She might not even believe it if I had evidence on film and a pack of nuns and Girl Scouts verifying your story. Caroline seems to have a perpetual get out of jail free card, and even if Harper does believe me, Dr. Cheats-a-lot will just talk her way out of it."

"But we need to do something, don't we?"

Emilia nodded again. "We do."

"And I think maybe I should go before they come back out. Tell Harper goodnight for me."

"I'm not delivering enough of your messages?" They shared a brief hug before she pushed her toward the door. "Get out of here. I'll let you know how it goes."

"Thanks, Emilia."

"What are you doing here?" Harper spun on Caroline as soon as the bedroom door closed behind them.

"Do I need a reason other than I wanted to see you?"

Caroline smiled her most charismatic smile, clearly trying to avoid the question. For possibly the first time ever, Harper failed to find it charming. "Yes, you do."

"Okay. Maybe I wanted to help you."

"You came to help?" She knew she looked as irritated as she sounded, but she didn't believe for one second that Caroline had suddenly found time in her busy schedule to begin volunteering for a cause she hadn't bothered to care about before her new volunteer showed up to threaten her security.

"Don't act so surprised. I've helped you before."

Now she was confused. "When, exactly, have you helped me?"

"Well, I've wanted to help."

"That's kind of different from actually doing so." She tried to keep the accusatory tone out of her voice. Judging by Caroline's expression, she wasn't successful. "I thought you had to work tonight."

"I moved some things around." She smiled broadly, claiming a victory that wasn't yet hers.

"For this you can move things around, but when I wanted you to go to dinner with my mother for her birthday, it was impossible to get out of work."

"I can't control when people need medical attention."

"Except for tonight, apparently."

Caroline unleashed an exasperated sigh, like she was the injured party. "I'm still on call, and there's a good chance I'll need to leave, possibly soon, but I decided I'd rather be here helping you, even for a few minutes, than anywhere else."

"I see. And what influenced this decision?"

"I just wanted to see you. That's all."

"Should I assume that all those other times you're on call and unavailable you don't want to see me?"

"What has gotten into you?"

"Nothing at all. I just find it curious that only now, after I told you about my new volunteer, who happens to be female, do you realize that you can be on call here with me just as easily as wherever you usually are. Seems like someone as smart as you could have figured that out a while ago."

"Fine. I was jealous and wanted to see this Eliot person, to reassure myself."

"So you belittle the work I'm doing by using it as a cover story."

"That's not what I was doing. Or at least that wasn't what I meant to do. I guess I wasn't thinking about how it would look to you. I'm sorry."

"I can forgive you, if you actually help out. But if you're just going to sit there glowering at Eliot and getting in the way, I'm kicking you out."

"I promise there will be no glowering or other interference. I'm not worried anymore now that I've seen her."

Harper should have been relieved, not only because Caroline didn't see Eliot as a threat but also because she didn't even think she had the potential to be. She should have let it rest there. But she didn't. "You don't think she's attractive?"

"You do?"

Too late, Harper realized her mistake. Of course Caroline would take what would otherwise be casual conversation in a threatening way. Unfortunately, Harper couldn't exactly deny it, not without making herself an even bigger liar. But she absolutely didn't want to introduce Caroline to a more legitimate basis for her jealous behavior.

"I don't think she's unattractive," Harper said. "I was trying to set her up with Emilia."

"I thought you liked her. Do you really want her to suffer?"

"You just got out of trouble, and now you're trying to get back in it?"

"Of course not. I'm glad you want to help Emilia find a girlfriend. I think that will be great for her. And us."

"Well, she's not interested."

"At last we have something in common."

"I think you'll really like her if you get to know her. Just try being nice and nonjudgmental. I think you have it in you."

"I'll try, but I'm not making any promises."

"Come on. You survived med school, and you don't think you can have a civil conversation with someone who's a little different from you? Just pay attention to what she says instead of what she looks like."

"Seems like a lot of work for someone who isn't going to be in our lives very long."

"What makes you say that?"

"Your fundraiser is in a few weeks. Do you really see yourself spending time with this woman after you don't have a shared goal?"

"I do. So far I like everything I know about Eliot. I think I'll be lucky if she still wants to be my friend." That was a bit of a stretch. Harper had no doubt Eliot still wanted to associate with her. Why else would she kick up her volunteer efforts? True, she claimed she was doing it to make up for the trouble she'd caused, but she could have offered to do any number of other things. Either she was duplicitous and still trying to foster a romance, or she liked spending time with her.

"So we're going to be palling around with the painted lady out there?"

"That seems doubtful. I can hardly get you to socialize with the friends I have now. I don't really expect you to suddenly get more sociable with new people. I just want you to be open to the possibility of her being around."

"Consider me open. I will play nice and try to see her the way you do."

Though Harper successfully stifled the flash of panic at that thought, she couldn't hide her disappointment that, while she'd been interrogating her girlfriend in private, Eliot had left her alone with Caroline and Emilia.

CHAPTER SEVENTEEN

"Good thing I showed up. Your help seems to have disappeared."

"Yeah. Good thing," Harper muttered, not certain it was a good thing at all.

She wanted to reach out to know what happened, but with Caroline attached to her side, she could hardly engage in a hearty text exchange with another woman. On top of that, she didn't have a surplus of time to spare—unlike Eliot, her work hadn't vanished. She still had so much to do and a disappointing lack of backup, and she didn't kid herself that Caroline would keep her word and help.

Thirty minutes later when, to no one's surprise, Caroline was called back to work, Harper was actually relieved. No longer would she have to divide her attention between her work and the demands of her excessively needy girlfriend. Caroline had spent the entire time bickering with Emilia, rather than actually advancing the cause, further emphasizing the loss of Eliot.

She tried to regroup once her non-helper left, but she could feel Emilia staring at her. Under normal circumstances, that was vexing, but when she was trying to wheedle funds for a non-glamorous cause from wealthy strangers, it was downright unnerving.

"Was there something you wanted to say?"

"Nothing you're going to want to hear."

"Let me guess. It's about Caroline." She could already hear the familiar anti-Caroline refrain and didn't really have time for another chorus, but she doubted Em's intense stare would go away until she unloaded her latest batch of insults. "You might as well go ahead. I promise I'm paying attention. It only looks like I'm writing an email."

"You can't be mad at me for telling you." She joined her at the kitchen table and held her hands, heightening the creepy intensity of the moment while seriously impeding her progress. "You have to remember that I tried to give you a way out."

"Your efforts were notable and impressive. It's amazing I wasn't swayed. Just tell me whatever it is that has you scowling at me so I can get back to work."

"Eliot left because of Caroline."

"That's ridiculous. She didn't even say hello."

"Apparently she didn't need to."

"This is so childish. I thought she was going to try to move past what happened."

"It's gotten more complicated."

"In the ten minutes we were out of the room it suddenly became complicated?"

"Stop interrupting and listen to me." Nervous, she waited for whatever was so important. "Eliot knows Caroline."

"Even weirder that she didn't stick around."

"Or not since she saw her cheating on you."

"What?" She rose abruptly and then sank back into her seat as the room tilted on its axis.

"She saw her kissing another woman."

"She's wrong."

"She was certain."

"And you believe her?"

"I have no reason not to."

"Well I do. She just wants to break us up."

"She thought you'd see it that way. That's why she asked me to tell you."

"Because you don't have the same agenda?"

"I would love it if you dumped her ass. But I don't need to make up stories to make that happen."

"No, you'll just repeat them."

"Why are you so sure it's not true?"

"Why are you so sure it is?"

"Other than the fact that your girlfriend can't be bothered to treat you with respect or common courtesy? I'm actually more surprised that I hadn't anticipated this, but if you're so sure it's not true, why don't you ask her?"

"I'm not going to accuse her of cheating on me just to satisfy your curiosity, especially not on the strength of the extremely biased source."

"Is that why? Or are you afraid to find out that your girlfriend isn't the god you thought she was?"

Her mouth opened, but words wouldn't come out. She was livid, but beneath the anger, there was part of her that wondered. What if it was true? But it couldn't be. She would know. Wouldn't she? If it was true, if there was even a hint of truth to that statement, what would that mean for them? For her? She'd been Caroline's girlfriend for so long. She didn't want to consider what it would mean to be something else.

Eliot didn't think she could maintain innocuous chatter with a well-meaning Uber driver, so she walked four blocks to the train, enjoying the calm night air and the quiet of the neighborhood. It was a stark contrast to her own inner turmoil, but the fact that she could still brush up against serenity even though she was light years from experiencing it herself was almost like relief.

She checked her phone repeatedly, though she knew Emilia hadn't yet had time to deliver the bad news, especially if they weren't alone. The conversation would be hard enough without the looming presence of the cheater herself. Twice Eliot almost turned back. She regretted foisting such an unpleasant but important mission on Emilia. It wasn't fair to make her the sole bearer of bad news. And Eliot wanted to help comfort Harper. Only the fear that she would be blamed and forbidden from any further contact kept her heading home, not that the backlash couldn't reach her there.

Her phone rang, cutting into her hearty self-flagellation.

"I know you're busy, and I don't want to interrupt," Georgie started.

"You aren't interrupting anything. I left early." She braced herself for good-natured taunting. Georgie wasn't one to let a rare lapse in her sister's cool pass without comment.

"You need to come." Though the train was loud, and her connection was quiet, the panic she heard in her sister's voice drowned out the roiling cacophony of a car full of Cubs fans. "We're back at the hospital. You need to come."

"I'm on my way." She pushed her way through the crowd, ready to jump off the train and run to the hospital if necessary. "Just tell her to hang on."

Unable to concentrate on anything other than Emilia's baseless accusation, Harper gave up on her work and retreated to her bedroom, but in spite of her best attempts to hide from her friend and every consequence associated with their conversation, the seed that Emilia had planted (thanks to Eliot) took root in her thoughts. She would be remiss if she didn't try to clear away these doubts, minuscule though they were. If she didn't talk to Caroline about it, the almost nonexistent possibility that Eliot was right would nag and grow until it drove them apart. She didn't want that. And what about Caroline? If she didn't give her the opportunity to defend herself, that would be unfair. She deserved to know what had been said about her, didn't she?

Beneath the war between doubt and loyalty, the latent notion of defining herself by her own accomplishments rather than by being an appendage to Caroline's took hold as well. More concerning, it gave her more satisfaction than she had ever thought possible. For a year now, she had been happy to be by her side and had taken pride in her girlfriend's achievements, proudly proclaiming them to anyone who would listen and even some who would have preferred not to.

But she was beginning to see that she had an impressive list of accomplishments as well. She was mad at Eliot, but she acknowledged that, without her and her generous appreciation for her work, she still might not have realized that she wasn't entirely unimpressive.

Still, she didn't have to break up with Caroline in order to achieve her full potential. Obviously, if Eliot saw something worthwhile in her, she was doing something right, and she'd been doing it as Caroline's girlfriend, not in spite of that. Unless she was fooling herself, she thought as she rolled over to stare at a different wall. Eliot was clearly biased and had an obvious get-in-her-pants agenda. Perhaps her opinion was not to be trusted any more than her stories of cheating girlfriends.

But were her pants really worth so much trouble to get into? This seemed like a lot of work if the end goal was just sex. So if it was more than that—if Eliot genuinely cared for her—then maybe it was worth considering what she'd told Em, which naturally led to considering the other ways in which Harper might have been fooling herself.

And just like that, the hint of doubt that her friends had introduced exploded into a profusion of incertitude.

CHAPTER EIGHTEEN

The light from the hallway seeped into the darkened room, casting a deceptively soothing glow on the family as they gathered around Audrey's bed. She'd been admitted just after nine, crushing all their hopes that she would sleep in her own bed that night. And though visiting hours were over and they all should have gone home to worry in their respective living spaces, none of the hospital staff came forward to enforce the rules and send them away. Maybe it was because they'd ingratiated themselves to the entire staff during Audrey's last hospitalization. Inspired by her inherent sweetness, they'd been unfailingly kind and respectful to every nurse they'd encountered, thus establishing themselves as favorites. Or maybe they were just so pathetic, huddled around her bed and watching her breathe that no one had the heart to tell them to leave. No matter the reason, by unspoken agreement, they kept quiet to avoid drawing attention to themselves and their illicit after-hours loitering. Every time a nurse passed the door, they all tensed in anticipation of their collective eviction, but thus far the full staff had taken pity on them.

Audrey had drifted off to sleep not long after settling in her room. The soft gurgling whir of the oxygen was the only sound as the five adults crowded together to watch her sleep. For several minutes, no one dared move for fear of waking her up, but at the sight of her chest rising and falling with her steady, even breaths, their vigilance relaxed ever so slightly.

"What happened with volunteering?" Georgie whispered. "Why did you leave early?" Though her question was directed at Eliot, Georgie's focus never left her daughter—in fact, the only part of her body that wasn't tuned to Audrey was the hand that clung to her husband's. This query, it seemed, served the dual purpose of satisfying her curiosity and providing an innocent (and likely fruitless) distraction.

"It got too crowded."

"Since when do you avoid crowds?"

"Since they include the girlfriend of the woman I'm pining for."

Her mother shifted in her seat but remained miraculously peripheral to their conversation.

"You didn't get into some weird, macho competitive thing with her, did you?" Georgie asked.

"That would have required spending more than thirty seconds in her presence."

"So you just bolted as soon as you laid eyes on her?"

"There might have been a five-minute gap in which I ratted her out as a cheater to Harper's best friend." Georgie's brow furrowed, and her mouth fell open. "Dr. West is the girlfriend, by the way."

That broke her sister's concentration on Audrey. "How is your love life so complicated that Audrey has gotten caught up in it?"

"If it's any consolation, I'm not sure how much longer that connection will last."

"Oh, yeah. I'm sure that will be a big help."

She jumped as the chirp of an incoming text broke the near silence, startling her and her family.

Can we talk? That was all Harper's message said. At any other time she would have rushed to call her. She was worried about her and what she was going through. To be honest, she was also worried about herself and whether she'd be blamed for the cheating she had no part in. Instead of calling, however, she merely silenced the phone and returned her attention to the sick little girl sound asleep in front of her.

"Is that her?" Georgie whispered.

"There's a *her*?" Her mother, apparently no longer able to restrain her meddling, finally joined the conversation. On a lone positive note, she sounded more hopeful than judgmental, but she was still hesitant. The number of girlfriends her mother had approved of could be counted on one finger.

"There's a hopeful her."

"Not if you ignore her, there isn't."

"It's more complicated than that, Ma."

"So tell me what's so complicated."

"This isn't the right time."

"If I wasn't here, if it was just you and your sister, would you talk about it?"

Eliot frowned but said nothing. She couldn't exactly deny it.

"We used to talk all the time. You used to tell me things. When did that change?"

"When you finally got the daughter you wanted with the man you prefer."

"Eliot," Georgie admonished, her stern gaze a warning. There was no scenario in which witnessing a fight between her grandmother and Zizi would benefit Audrey. She took a deep breath and apologized to her stunned mother. Then, remembering Georgie's request that she have a real conversation with her, she regrouped and decided to try a different approach. "The hospital cafeteria sells battery acid disguised as coffee. Can I buy you a cup?"

"I'm fine."

"Are you sure? Maybe we could talk."

Her mother sat silently for a moment, stretching Eliot's discomfort to its limits, until Georgie pointedly cleared her throat, and her mother said, "On second thought, I'm overdue for an assault on my taste buds. I'll walk with you."

Despite the intended goal of their outing, neither of them spoke as they made their way to the cafeteria with its harsh lights and total lack of warmth. And even after they sat across a table from one another, their chairs almost as uncomfortable as the silence, it took a few moments for Eliot to gather the courage to say what her mother needed to hear. "Do you remember the last good conversation we had?"

She frowned in concentration but came up short. "I can't say I do. It's been a while."

"I think I was in high school."

"So what happened to us? How did we get here?"

"There were a lot of little disagreements along the way, but I think college is when it got too big to ignore."

"You didn't go to college."

"You mean I didn't go to the college you wanted me to, so you refused to pay for it." Somehow she kept the familiar anger from her voice. She wasn't sure her mother would appreciate how hard she was trying.

"We wanted you to get a real degree."

"I have a real degree, Mom. A Bachelor of Arts is a real degree that I had to work hard to earn and that you've never once been proud of me for." Her phone vibrated again, and again she ignored it. "Do you not see how much it hurts me when you're so dismissive?"

"It's not dismissive. It's protective."

"What are you protecting me from? A mother who loves me?"

"You think I don't love you? Why would you think I don't love you?"

"Maybe because you don't act like you do. You criticize everything I do so much that sometimes I'm not sure you even like me."

"Have you never wondered why?"

"I've wondered my whole life." Her voice broke and she felt tears threatening.

"When you came out, I was so scared for you. I thought you'd be on your own. I know that's foolish of me, but back then, marriage wasn't a possibility for you, and I worried that without a spouse to help carry the burden, to take care of you, your life would be a constant struggle. But if you had a steady job in a solid industry, if you could provide your own financial stability, it would be okay. So I tried to push you into a field that could give you what you wouldn't get from a husband. I was trying to take care of you."

Although that was the most sweetly objectionable thing Eliot had ever heard, she didn't even resist the impulse to hug her mother. She moved to her side of the table, wrapped her arms around her and immediately felt the embrace tighten.

After a moment, she leaned far enough back to look in her mother's eyes while still holding onto her. "Ma, I know you don't believe it, but I promise you I'm fine. I love my job, and I'm really good at it, one of the best. And even though it's taking a while to establish that fact, my future in this industry is undeniable. The industry itself is undeniable. I'll be all right." She squeezed her once more for good measure. "And if it makes you feel any better, I tend bar because I like it. It's fun for me. You really don't need to worry about me."

It took almost a minute for her mother to release her hold and break her silence. "But don't you want a partner? Someone to share all this success and happiness with? Preferably someone who wants children?"

"I do. Except for maybe that last part."

She gestured with her chin at Eliot's buzzing phone. "Then you should call that young lady who keeps trying to talk to you."

"She has a girlfriend."

"And I had a husband when I met your stepfather. Things change."

Eliot shook her head at all the unexpected turns the evening had taken. She kissed her mother's cheek and stood, wondering if there would be one more unlikely twist, and then went in search of an inconspicuous place to make a phone call.

Harper glanced out her bedroom window, but thanks to the clouds obscuring the minimal light from the sliver of moon, she couldn't see much. Recognizing the lamentable similarities between her current view and the miserable, uncertain state of her love life, she pulled the curtains closed and sat on her bed. She'd long ago given up on falling to sleep. No matter how hard she tried, she couldn't seem to do anything other than worry about Caroline and whoever else she'd been kissing. Or maybe kissing. She still didn't know what to believe. Em seemed positive, but it would be about as difficult to convince her of Caroline doing something wrong as it would be to persuade her to try an all wine and chocolate diet. Not that she thought her friend would lie to her, at least not intentionally.

But Em might repeat a lie if it was compelling enough, and considering her hobby of fault-finding where Caroline was concerned, any story about her misbehavior would be compelling. So the real question was whether or not she trusted Eliot. Up until tonight, she would have said she did, or at least that she had no reason not to. She had seemed earnest and kind and compassionate, not the sort of woman to deceive and manipulate others to satisfy her own desires.

But she had obvious motivation to lie. Why wouldn't she try to get rid of what stood between her and what she wanted? What did she have to lose by maligning Caroline's character? She didn't want to believe she could be that duplicitous and cavalier about another person's reputation, but she hadn't known her that long. She had no way of knowing she wasn't a compulsive liar.

It would probably help to talk to Eliot directly. Then she could get a sense of whether she was telling the truth, or if Em had misinterpreted what she'd said. If she heard the story firsthand rather than through the filter of her best friend's contempt, she could tell the fact from the fiction. At least that's what she told herself as she reached for her phone.

She knew it was late—too late to call, but she couldn't wait until morning. She needed some kind of answers, and the potential peace of mind was too alluring to allow politeness to sway her. She had to have answers and Eliot could provide them.

Deciding that a text was marginally more considerate than a phone call, she opted to send a quick message asking if they could talk. She didn't have to answer if she was sleeping. Or heartless. Or busy sabotaging yet another relationship.

But when she hadn't gotten a response fifteen minutes later, she completely disregarded her earlier campaign for courtesy and sent a second, more urgent text (complete with liberal use of exclamation points): *Please call me! I need to talk to you! It's urgent!* Surely Eliot would know she was in agony and put her out of her misery. She wouldn't make her wait until morning to have this conversation. That would be unfair—almost as bad as a cowardly, second-party accusation of infidelity.

But after another five silent and agonizingly long minutes passed, it seemed as if she would have to wait. Still, one more text wouldn't hurt. Just a simple, direct, emphatic all caps plea for communication. She wouldn't keep ignoring her if she knew how important this was.

Assuming that Eliot would be no more considerate or responsive to that text (despite the obvious magnitude of the situation), she opted to stew angrily in the relative comfort of her bed. She would wait impatiently for some kind of response. Or at least until morning. On the off chance that she decided to quit being a self-absorbed mythomaniac, she kept her phone within reach then shut her eyes tightly and willed sleep to come. She was on the verge of sending one final last-ditch message when her phone rang.

"You need to tell me everything."

Harper's voice was hard-edged and harsh, and she didn't bother with pleasantries. In fact, nothing about her in this moment could be considered pleasant, and already Eliot regretted taking her mother's advice.

"What did you say to Emilia? What did you see? I need to know everything."

"What did she tell you?"

"That you accused Caroline of cheating on me."

"Then you already do know everything."

"I need to hear it for myself."

"So you can judge if I'm lying?"

"I just need to know what you saw. *Please*."

She knew she should be sympathetic. She'd faced similar circumstances, and though it had been a challenge, ultimately, she appreciated learning the truth. Now, however, even though she knew that Harper would eventually benefit from this moment, she didn't relish the role of Band-aid ripping truth-teller. Nevertheless, she relented and shared the unsavory details of the brief but damning scene she'd witnessed. Despite her desire to soften the story to spare Harper's feelings, she didn't hold back. Maybe the unsparing honesty would help.

"Unbelievable."

"I know it's hard to accept—"

"Not her. You."

"What?"

"I know you would prefer if I was single, but that doesn't mean you should make up stories about my girlfriend. And on top of that, you used Allies as a way to get to me. Do you know how hurtful that is? Do you even care about the work I'm doing? Or the people I've helped? How can you think this is okay? I can't believe I trusted you when all you wanted was to get Caroline out of the way."

"Harper, that's—"

"And then to ignore me. You had to have known I would need to talk, that I would want answers, but you couldn't even be bothered to acknowledge me. I thought you were a decent person, but you're not. You're selfish, and you don't care that you're hurting other people. Do you have anything to say for yourself?"

"I was just calling to tell you that I can't talk right now because I'm at the hospital."

"What?" Her voice sounded ten thousand times smaller.

"I was going to suggest that we talk tomorrow when my niece is, hopefully, stable, but even if she is, I'm really not sure I'll be up for another round of being your proxy punching bag." She hung up without giving her a chance to respond.

CHAPTER NINETEEN

"Jesus!" Em jumped when she spotted Harper sitting in the dark of their living room. "What are you doing out here?"

Sometime after Eliot's phone call—the call that made her feel like a selfish ass on top of being upset, angry and confused—she'd abandoned her bedroom to see if the couch could improve her chances of falling asleep. It hadn't, but the change in scenery was refreshing. And it didn't hurt that Em's cats viewed her as an optimal napping space. Though they'd repeatedly jabbed her full bladder with their paws, their soft purrs as she stroked their fur and stared at the wall helped offset the mounting irritation of turmoil-induced insomnia.

"I couldn't sleep."

"Because of Caroline?"

"Because of Eliot, actually." At Em's silent, raised-eyebrow request for information, Harper shared the details of her disastrous phone call, ending with the powerful anger-confusion-embarrassment combo she was currently failing to sort out. "I just don't know why she would do this. I get that she likes me, but why would she lie about Caroline like that? Why couldn't she just be my friend?"

"I think you're missing the part where she was being an amazing friend. There's a big difference between you refusing to believe something and that thing being a lie."

"Of course you're on her side. You've never liked Caroline."

"Only because she's never given me any reason to."

"We're never going to agree on this."

"Not before I have to go to work anyway." She offered the olive branch of a fresh cup of coffee before leaving her alone in the dark of the room and her thoughts.

"We need to talk."

Emilia held a box of donuts in one hand and a cup of coffee in the other. Her expression was full of eager impatience, like she was waiting for Eliot to understand the far-from-obvious explanation for her crush's best friend's presence in her niece's hospital room. Beyond confused, she gratefully accepted the cup of coffee but couldn't seem to form the words to ask what was happening.

Audrey smiled from her bed, attracting their surprise visitor's pleased attention. "You're the donut lady. You're pretty. As pretty as your donuts."

"And as the only person ever to recognize that fact, you get free donuts for life." She handed the box to the little girl. "I need to borrow your aunt for a few minutes. Is that all right?" Audrey nodded vigorously, her teeth already sinking into what appeared to be the chocolatiest chocolate donut in the history of chocolate's relationship with breakfast. Emilia smiled her thanks, waved a wordless and belated greeting to Eliot's stunned and miraculously silent family, and then dragged her into the hallway.

"What are you doing here?"

"I told you. We need to talk."

Eliot had actually been expecting Em to reach out. She just hadn't anticipated that it would be in person. "But how did you know where to find me?"

"Harper told me about your niece. You told me about her doctor, and I've heard all about which hospital she works at, so here I am." They moved their conversation closer to the elevators, away from the staff and other patients.

"We need to do something about Harper."

"I tried. It went over about as well as George Clooney's Batman."

"We just have to convince her that her girlfriend is cheating scum."

"I'm pretty sure she doesn't want to be convinced."

"Of course she doesn't. It's not about what she wants. It's about what needs to happen."

Not knowing which was more ill-advised—trying to convince Harper that her girlfriend was a gross womanizer not to be trusted, or trying to argue with Emilia that they couldn't force her to believe the truth—she decided it was easier just to hear Em out. "What do you have in mind?"

"If we could find out where she lives—"

"Doesn't Harper have her address?"

"She's never been to her house."

"And she didn't find that suspicious?"

"Not for lack of effort on my part." She allowed herself the luxury of one hearty sigh. "Anyway, if we find out where she lives, we can get evidence that she's cheating."

"What are we going to do? Hide behind a lamppost and hope she brings a date home for us to photograph? How is the world's most poorly planned stakeout going to help us?"

"Okay, so I hadn't thought that all the way through. She might not bring the other woman home, but she has a roommate. We could talk to her."

"And say what? That we're census takers with some wildly inappropriate questions? Don't you think this is a little extreme?"

"It's a lot extreme. This is an extreme situation. My best friend is being taken advantage of, and she's completely blind to it. Willingly so. I can't let her be hurt more than she already has been. So yeah, I'm suggesting some extreme measures."

Eliot slumped against the wall and closed her eyes. This was ridiculous and far more trouble than it was worth. Harper had made her choice. She wanted to believe her girlfriend. She preferred to dwell in blissful ignorance instead of facing the pain of dealing with the truth. Why should Eliot go so very far out of her way to force that truth on her, especially when she'd made it so clear that wasn't what she wanted?

Because she liked her. She liked her a lot, and despite her extreme but somewhat understandable selfishness the previous night, Eliot still didn't want to see her hurt. And, she reminded herself again, the benefit of facing this kind of truth didn't come without a healthy dose of discomfort. She hadn't had the luxury of denial, what with the literal naked truth confronting her in her own bed. But if there had been room for denial, would she have embraced it like Harper had? She didn't know, but she did know that she was better off for getting past her ex's transgressions. She hoped Harper would be as well. Besides, it's what Kate Bishop would do.

"Okay," she said, still not fully believing what she was agreeing to. "We'll find her address and figure out how to prove she cheated."

"How do we start?"

"I know someone who might be willing to help."

Hours later, as she lurked in the physicians' area of the parking garage, she again second-guessed her decision-making. This was never going to work. And even if it did, what then? How would they go from getting an address to getting proof? Neither one of them had the time to follow Caroline until she had another date with the other woman, if she even did. What if that was a one-time thing?

Just then, she spotted Caroline emerging from the elevator, and feeling even more ridiculous, she ducked behind a nearby cement column. *Please let this work*, she thought as she watched Caroline's journey to her BMW. "Of course," Eliot groaned, watching from her hiding place as Caroline took three years to fasten her seat belt and start the car. "I'm surprised she doesn't have vanity plates," she muttered, snapping pictures as the doctor drove away. Feeling more ridiculous by the second, she called her old friend.

"Alice. I need a favor."

CHAPTER TWENTY

"Before I give this to you, what do you plan to do with it?" Alice stood in her entryway, hands on hips, waiting to be convinced that she wasn't contributing to a very bad plan. If only Eliot could offer that reassurance.

"To be honest, I'm not sure. We really hadn't thought that far in advance."

"Who's we? Is it Lainie's friend from work? I knew you two would hit it off."

Alice sauntered into the room and dropped herself onto the couch, ready for whatever explanation was forthcoming. Apparently her minor abuse of power was more palatable if it helped pave the way to romance for her friend. To her credit, she refrained from eyebrow wiggling and all other overt displays of juvenile interest.

"It's actually her best friend, Emilia." Eliot handed Alice a beer without bothering to ask if she wanted it. "We're sort of trying to convince Harper that her girlfriend is cheating scum."

"So that you can be with her. Drastic measures, but I can support this."

"It's not a scheme to clear a path for my romantic plans. Her girlfriend really is cheating scum. Harper just doesn't want to believe it. So we're trying to convince her."

"And what makes you think this is a good idea? I remember when you had cheating scum of your own. You weren't exactly happy to share that news with others. Why do you think Harper wants not only to have her relationship violently torn apart, but also to suffer the same humiliation you tried to avoid at all costs?"

"I'm not trying to humiliate her. Believe me, I'm sensitive to what she's feeling. Or will be if she ever believes it. Denial appears to be her superpower."

"You could just let her keep believing what she wants to. This is a lot of effort for someone who might never appreciate it."

"That's a possibility, but I know I'm better off for having learned the truth. I think Harper will be too."

"Because then you can have a shot with her?"

"No." Alice's eyebrows shot to her hairline. "I mean, yes, I have feelings for her, but that's not why I'm doing this. I know my motives seem suspicious. I'd question them too if I were you. But I promise, I just don't want her to keep being hurt by someone who doesn't care about her like I—like she should."

"Okay." She handed her a folded sheet of paper and waited for her to take it all in. She read the information three times over, certain she was imagining things.

"Wait a minute. What? Does this say what I think it says?"

"If you think it says that the car is registered to Caroline West and Eileen Hampton-West, then yes, it says exactly that."

"She's married?"

"It sure seems that way. Unless she has a stepsister who shares her home and car as well as, in part, her last name."

"This is so much worse than I thought. I thought she was just seeing someone on the side. And I guess she is, but it's Harper."

"Are you going to go over there and do something stupid? Do I need to remind you that you aren't really in a comic book?

And just because you're friends with a cop, that doesn't mean you won't end up in prison."

"I appreciate the reminder. The chance of me doing something stupid is always high, but no, I don't think I have to now."

"What does that mean? What are you thinking?"

"Mostly I'm thinking I won't have to hide in her bushes now."

"Do I even want to know?"

"Probably better if you don't. I have to share this with Emilia." She reached for her phone, her heart racing as she searched for her coconspirator's number. "We need to tell Harper."

"Just be gentle with her. She's not getting the irrefutable visual evidence you experienced, but this is still going to be a shock. Give her time to accept it. And then ask her out because you two should absolutely be a couple."

"You saw us together once."

"Some of us are more observant than others. Now go call your accomplice."

Harper lay on the couch, reading her book and pointedly ignoring her roommate, a.k.a., the traitor and originator of her current inner turmoil. True, that would have been easier to accomplish if she'd retreated to her bedroom as her exhaustion compelled her to, but then Em wouldn't know she was being ignored. And if she didn't know, then what was the point?

She read the same sentence for the fourth time, no closer to comprehending it, as snippets of the phone conversation she definitely wasn't eavesdropping on caught her attention. On the surface, the seemingly innocuous comments she latched onto could have been about anything. Phrases like, "Did you get it?" and "That can't be right," and "Text it to me" weren't particularly interesting or damning. But when followed with a somber, "No, I'll take care of it," they suddenly took on a menacing air. Not that she cared.

That the subject of this discussion was more than likely her relationship with Caroline was even more reason to maintain her campaign of forced disinterest. Either she was wrong and had learned nothing from the previous night's sterling example of self-absorption, or she was right, and the evening would end in an argument. She'd had more than enough arguing lately. With that in mind, she forced herself to focus on the formerly compelling pages of *Becoming*. She got one sentence further before she was interrupted by the sustained and increasingly pointed clearing of Em's throat.

"Do you need a lozenge?" She refused to look away from her book.

"No. I need to tell you something you don't want to hear."

"But that's what you did last night." She turned the page in spiteful defiance of her near reverse progress with this chapter.

"You were right that Caroline wasn't cheating on you." Now she did look up, smug expression on full display, ready to enjoy the view as Em feasted on her own words and Eliot's. Finally, she would get some relief from the near-constant Caroline bashing. It was almost worth the unpleasantness of the past twenty-four hours just to reach this minor milestone. "She was cheating with you."

"What?"

"Caroline is married."

"You're wrong."

What else could she say? Was she really supposed to believe that she'd paid so little attention to the woman she'd been sleeping with for a year that she'd missed this substantial bit of information? None of this made sense.

"I wish I were. Eliot just told me—"

"Well, if Eliot told you, then it must be true. She would never lie, would she? If I didn't believe that Caroline kissed another woman, why would I believe this?"

"Because there's proof." Even in the face of her escalating outrage, Em managed to keep her voice calm, which only agitated Harper more.

"Show me. Where is it?" she challenged, still certain she was right, still sure this was nothing more than jealousy and wishful thinking on her tormentors' part. But that certainty faded as she stared at the picture on her friend's phone. "What's this?"

"It's the registration information on Caroline's car. I guess Eliot knows someone who could run the plates."

"You stalked her?"

"For the greater good."

"But this doesn't have to mean she's married," she sputtered, the fight dying as numbness overtook her. "So she co-owns a car with someone who has the same last name. That doesn't automatically make," she stared harder at the picture, "Eileen her wife." She gagged on the word.

"Why don't you ask her?"

"Just call her up and say, 'You wouldn't happen to be married, would you? Just curious'?"

"Or ask her who Eileen is."

"This just can't be true."

"Find out for sure. Ask her. But do me a favor and ask her when I'm around to witness it. She has a track record of talking herself out of everything, and you have a habit of believing anything she says."

"No matter what she says, you're automatically going to think it's a lie."

"I promise to be objective." She favored her with an incredulous glare. "Mostly because I don't believe that even she could dream up a lie big enough to explain this away. But if she does, if she offers an even halfway believable explanation, I promise that I will never say anything negative about her for the rest of my life. I'll go out of my way to be nice to her. I'll bake her an apology cake. That's how sure I am about this."

"Can I get that in writing?"

"I'll have it notarized if you want."

In the face of Em's conviction, Harper's own certainty dimmed. She still didn't believe it. When it came to Caroline's character and behavior, Em's beliefs were hardly the standard by which to set her own. There simply had to be some other explanation. On the surface, though, this did seem to be damning evidence. But if they were wrong, she would start an argument for nothing, and there was no doubt a loaded accusation like this would end in a fight. No matter what Caroline's answer was, she would resent being asked. So what could Harper live with: Caroline's anger or Harper's own doubt coupled with her roommate's persistence? Because just like Caroline's anger, Em's refusal to drop this was guaranteed.

Neither option was ideal, but at least if she asked, she would eventually find peace of mind. Apprehensive and not at all sure she was making the right decision, she reached for her phone.

"I need to see you. Can you come over?"

CHAPTER TWENTY-ONE

Though Caroline had promised she would come as soon as she could get away, until their buzzer broke the uncomfortable silence in the apartment, Harper hadn't fully expected her to keep her word. That in itself was a fairly clear indication that, even if their relationship wasn't a lie, it was far from perfect. Further evidence (that she didn't particularly want to acknowledge) was the effort she'd had to exert just to see her. Instead of rushing over or even saying that she'd love to see her but just couldn't make it happen tonight, she'd seemed put out, like it was a burden or a trial to see her girlfriend on a Tuesday night.

"It's sort of an emergency," she'd told her, feeling only slightly guilty about stretching the truth, and when it worked, she felt both vindicated and disheartened. Now that she was here, rushing to take care of her in her hour of need, she just felt hollow.

"What's wrong? What happened?" She cupped her face, scrutinizing her appearance, her frenzied concern making it impossible to ask the question she'd called her here to answer. "You scared me on the phone. Tell me what's going on."

"I need to ask you something." She spoke tentatively, being careful to get this right.

"It must be one hell of a question if you made me race over here to answer it." A gentle smile (did it seem nervous?) softened the criticism.

"You're not wrong," Emilia muttered, earning a dual glare.

"I need to ask you, who is Eileen Hampton-West?"

The color drained from Caroline's face, her mouth fell open, and for a moment, Harper worried she'd have to catch her unconscious soon-to-be ex-girlfriend. But Caroline steadied herself against the wall, and gave a short, sharp laugh.

"You didn't answer the question." Though her reaction should have been torturous confirmation enough, she needed to hear it. "Who is she?"

"You already know. What do you want me to say?"

"I want you to tell me it's not true." The words barely squeaked past the lump of hurt and anger in her throat.

Unbelievably, she looked like the picture of poise and innocence, like she had no idea that bad things happened in this world or that she could ever be at the heart of them.

But she didn't deny it.

"How long have you been married?"

"Five years, but we've been together almost sixteen."

The air left her lungs, and her vision blurred, but she refused to sink to the floor as her suddenly weak knees wanted her to do. She felt a steadying hand on her arm and pushed it away.

"Don't touch me."

Caroline's hands flew up defensively, and she backed away. "Don't be angry with me."

"Don't be angry with you? That's what you say when you have one too many cocktails with dinner or you forget to buy toilet paper. This is so much worse than that."

"I know it seems bad, but—"

"It doesn't *seem* bad, Caroline. It *is* bad."

"All I did was fall in love with you."

"No. All you did was turn me into your unwitting mistress."

She felt hot tears rolling down her cheeks and wiped them angrily away. "When I heard that you cheated on me, I thought it couldn't possibly be true. It doesn't feel as good as I thought it would to be right."

"Nothing has changed."

"Everything has, Caroline."

"Can you honestly say you don't love me anymore?"

"I can honestly say it doesn't matter. I'm not willing to be your mistress."

"So I'll get a divorce."

"How is that a solution? Don't you even care about the woman you allegedly loved enough to marry? Doesn't it matter to you how you've treated her?"

"I never meant to hurt her. I just couldn't resist you."

"It was undeniable attraction. That's your excuse? That's supposed to make this okay?"

"I'm just being honest with you."

"It's about a year too late for that."

"I'm sorry for lying. I never meant to hurt anyone. It's not like I set out to have an affair. But you can't help who you fall for." She shrugged, as if to suggest that none of this was really her fault.

"I suppose you can't." She looked suddenly hopeful, like she thought she might somehow avoid a breakup. "But you can help who you sleep with." Harper opened the door wide, signaling that Caroline should make her exit. "And I won't make this mistake again."

Eliot knew it would take time to break the news to Harper, even longer for her to believe it, so she tried to distract herself. She prolonged Alice's stay with a thousand questions about her job and Lainie and an offer of dinner, but throughout their time together, she kept close watch on her phone. Surely Emilia would have told her by now. She wouldn't have waited until tomorrow. And how long would it take? Apparently a millennium. Her total lack of focus was further exacerbated by concern for Audrey. True, she seemed to be improving, but that had also been the case when she was released from the hospital less than a week earlier. How could they trust that this time was any different?

Once Alice left (following a stern reminder that the information on the license plate definitely had not come from her), Eliot resorted to work as a distraction. She'd allowed herself to fall behind again, though not quite as drastically as during Audrey's first hospitalization, when she'd kept a helpless vigil by her bedside. Yet her focus continuously drifted to her still silent phone and persistent thoughts of the many women in her life who were at a crossroads.

Eventually, she abandoned her paid work. She still had some catching up to do, but given the recent scare and all the implications that she refused to vocalize, she wanted to make progress on her niece's book while she was still here to enjoy it. At that thought, her throat tightened, and her gathering tears blurred her vision. She wanted to throw things and shout about how unfair this was. But who would listen?

Instead, she poured herself a drink, tamped down the emotions she'd kept at bay for weeks and forced herself to focus on the shape-shifting, time-traveling, atonement-seeking, fictionally bad-ass version of her niece. The more she drew, the more the story came to life for her, and she felt herself getting lost in it. The outside world, with its lies and manipulation and stupid fucking cancer, gradually retreated as Super Audrey (better name still pending) battled against admittedly less formidable foes than what real life Audrey faced.

She was just about to vanquish her nemesis when the chime of her phone broke the spell she'd cast for herself. It was after two in the morning, and her back and shoulders ached from the hours she'd spent hunched over her drafting table. She rubbed her suddenly tired eyes, trying to adjust to see the words on the small glowing screen. Apparently Harper wasn't having any more luck sleeping than she was.

I'm sorry I didn't believe you. I need a little time, but maybe we can talk?

I'd like that.

CHAPTER TWENTY-TWO

Three days passed before Harper had the nerve to follow through on her intention to talk with Eliot. Every time she considered what Eliot and her family were dealing with—what she'd thoughtlessly intruded upon in her own selfish stupidity—a fresh wave of shame washed over her. When she thought about how she'd treated Eliot in the completely undeserved defense of a woman who had made a career out of lying to her, she wondered just how awful life under a rock would be. She was beyond embarrassed, and if time machines were a real thing, she knew exactly how she'd put one to use.

Aside from Em, who'd thus far been a gloat-free witness, she'd told no one but her mother about the breakup. Her own mortification had been the primary roadblock to her candidness, but the extreme confusion she felt didn't help matters. How was she supposed to talk about something she still found so confounding? To say that a heart-to-heart with her mother didn't ease her bewilderment was an understatement.

"I hate to see you so broken up about this." She'd nudged the hot tea (in her mother's view, essentially panacea in beverage form) closer.

"Should I be happy about it like you and Em are?"

"Sweetie, I'm not happy that you're hurting."

"But you hated Caroline." She wrapped her hands around the mug, and in defiance of all logic, felt marginally better.

"I didn't hate her. I just wanted better for you."

"Better than a doctor?"

"Better than an excuse disguised as a relationship." She felt her jaw drop, but her mother disregarded her shock. Apparently it was brutal honesty week. "I know you convinced yourself that you loved Caroline. You stayed with her longer than any of your other girlfriends, but I think what you really loved was the convenience of her."

"Yeah, it was super convenient to have a girlfriend who was never available."

"When you consider that you could claim to be in a relationship without any of the real work or commitment involved, it was exactly what you needed. She was there when you wanted her and too busy with her own life to burden you with it. So you got all of the fun parts of a relationship—the romance and sex." She felt her face turn crimson at the sound of the word "sex" leaving her mother's mouth. "But you didn't have to deal with any of the hard stuff that makes a relationship challenging but also rewarding."

"And why would I do that?"

"Sweetheart, you lost so much so soon. It's a wonder you've taken the minor risks you have. Ever since Blake died, you've been determined not to hurt like that again. And for you the only way to avoid that is just not to love anyone. When you love someone fully, with every part of you, there's always the risk of being hurt. But shutting yourself off like you have? You'll never experience the joy and love I got from your father and brother. Nothing has hurt me like losing them. But even if that pain is the price I had to pay, I wouldn't give up the time I had with them. Not for anything, not even the assurance that I'll never hurt like that again."

While time with her mother had dulled the ache somewhat, it had done little to abate her emotional ambiguity. All her mother's praise of the joys of certain heartbreak aside, now, as she mustered up the courage to face the woman who'd launched her uncertainty, all she wanted to do was hide.

Eliot checked her watch and sighed. She'd agreed to meet Harper for A Very Important Conversation, but as much as she wanted to see her and reestablish some kind of friendship (she wouldn't let herself hope for more), she didn't want to leave Audrey's hospital room. Logically she understood that her physical proximity affected Audrey's wellness about as much as the color of her socks did. That still didn't mean she felt good about being elsewhere. On top of that, there was no way that Georgie wouldn't notice and weigh in on her atypically early departure.

Bracing herself for the inevitable commentary, Eliot rose from the seat she'd occupied for the past seven hours, grabbed her bag and announced her intention to leave before being kicked out by sternly sympathetic staff.

Georgie looked from her sister to the sunlight streaming through the window. "You realize it's still daylight, don't you?"

Eliot scowled but said nothing.

"If this is for a date, I approve."

Audrey, currently enjoying life without an oxygen mask, looked up from her coloring book to beam at her aunt. "Me too, Zizi."

"It's not a date. Harper wants to talk, and… I don't know what it is, but it's not a date."

"Okay, but I feel like your 'not a date' is somehow tied to our favorite doctor's current bad mood."

"She's your favorite doctor now?"

"Questionable dating practices aside, I like her. She's a great doctor. Look how well Audrey's doing." Eliot had to admit her niece looked about five thousand times healthier than she had upon her return to the hospital. Eliot wasn't willing to believe that any other doctor couldn't have achieved the same results, but it hadn't been any other doctor. It had been creepy Dr. West. "And I asked about..." She pointed to the tiny swell of her abdomen.

"What was the verdict on that?"

"She wouldn't tell me that I had nothing to worry about, but she said that we're not necessarily doomed to go through this again. So I feel better, at least when I let myself believe her."

"Risky move," she muttered.

"I know you don't like her, but she has done a lot for us."

"It's so unfair that she's made it impossible to hate her completely." Not that she'd rather have the liberty to fully despise the woman who was actively saving her niece's life.

"I'm sure your non-date hates her enough for both of you."

But thirty minutes later, upon seeing Harper standing uncertainly in her hallway, Eliot wasn't sure hatred was the prevailing emotion. Her first thought was that Harper didn't want to be there. Even though she'd initiated this meeting, everything from her downcast eyes to her poised-for-flight stance proclaimed her desire to be Anywhere But Here. In spite of her obvious discomfort, Harper stepped inside, accepted the drink she was offered and made it through the mindless small talk while they settled themselves on the couch. Whatever this was about, it was important enough for her to punish herself to get through it.

"I guess I should start by saying I'm sorry."

"You already did that."

"In that case, I'll say thank you. Who knows how long that would have continued? I'm just so embarrassed." The tears started falling and Harper looked away.

"You don't need to be embarrassed. You did nothing but fall in love with someone who didn't deserve it."

"I can't believe I didn't know. How could I not know she had this whole other life? How could I be so blind?"

"Because you were in love." Eliot laid a comforting hand on her arm.

"Was I? I thought so. Who wouldn't be in love with her?"

Eliot wisely kept her mouth shut. This wasn't the time to pick apart her ex.

"She's gorgeous and a doctor," Harper added.

"Doesn't make her a good person."

"She saves kids with cancer. She keeps parents from burying their children. That's not what a bad person does."

"I am undeniably grateful to every doctor, nurse, orderly, ambulance driver and anyone else who has helped keep Audrey alive. They are all incredibly good at their jobs, and because of their dedication, I still have my niece. At least for now. But being good at their jobs, no matter how important those jobs might be, doesn't give them a free pass on decency. Caroline may be the best pediatric oncologist in the galaxy—my sister certainly thinks so—but she treated you unfairly. She used you and lied to you, and for me, that outweighs what she does for a living. No amount of good work makes up for that. So don't defend her, and don't you dare feel bad about being mad at her. I know I am."

Harper wiped tears from her cheeks and offered a weak smile. "Thank you." She threw her arms around Eliot and hugged her tight. Though she enjoyed the closeness, she knew better than to believe it meant more than friendly gratitude.

Leaning back, Eliot looked into her expressive, vulnerable eyes. Her gaze drifted down to her full lips, and fighting the magnetic pull she felt, she cleared her throat and said the first thing that popped in her mind. "You probably didn't get much work done on the fundraiser the past few days."

"Try none. I feel like I went backward."

"So let me help."

"You'd be willing to do that?"

"It would be pretty foolish of me to offer if I wasn't."

"Why are you being so nice to me?"

"Why do you think you don't deserve it?"

"Recent behavior stands out."

"You had a bad day." She shrugged. "I can forgive that."

CHAPTER TWENTY-THREE

The dense language of the vendor contract Harper stared at made even less sense the second time she tried to find the answer she was looking for. Rather than taking a third pass, she let herself be distracted by the woman at the table beside her. This was the tenth time in three weeks that Eliot had come over to help her.

"Just until you're caught up," she'd say before dedicating the better part of her night to whatever tasks Harper needed done.

While it seemed highly unlikely that she had nothing better to do with her time, her assistance was invaluable. It also didn't hurt that she was a fun (if distracting) assistant.

During their last work session, she'd stopped what she was doing to rub Harper's tense, hunched shoulders. Her hands had roamed into her hair and down her back, sending shivers along her entire body and eliciting a satisfied moan that she couldn't contain if her mother's life depended on it. That had signaled the end of the impromptu massage, but not her lingering thoughts about Eliot's hands and all the other places she wanted to feel them.

But even just sitting there, she drew attention to herself. For one thing, she tended to play with any nearby writing utensils. Unless she was actively using her hands to work, the nearest pen or pencil started bouncing back and forth. And when she concentrated, she bit her bottom lip, drawing undue attention to an area that was already difficult to ignore. Harper looked instead at the small, inexplicably adorable crease in her brow as her eyes darted from computer screen to the file folder of papers between them. And in a truly damning turn of events, she smelled incredible.

"Eyes on your own paper." Eliot cast a sideways glance at her, a move that was somehow more alluring than her full gaze.

"I just want to make sure you don't need anything."

"I need my pushy boss to remember that she already spent two hours explaining the extreme importance of logging every donation in the spreadsheet. She even printed a reference guide so that I put the correct information in the right little rectangles."

"Cells. They're called cells." She pointed to the word in the instructions she'd provided.

"Will it throw off the results if I don't use the proper terminology?"

"Unquestionably so."

"I'm going to go ahead and throw caution to the wind on this."

"And endanger the data?"

"You know, I don't have to stay."

"No. I want you here."

"Good. I want me here too." Their eyes met for a charged minute before Eliot looked back to her work. "Where should we eat tonight?"

It had become part of their ritual to cap off a night of hard volunteering with dinner, almost always from the Mediterranean restaurant across the street, but as much as she enjoyed the expansive falafel and hummus offerings, she wondered if Eliot wanted something new.

"Head volunteer's choice." She tried a wink and wasn't at all disappointed when Eliot completely missed her awkward attempt.

"What? Allowing liberties with the little rectangles and now this? I'll soon be drunk with power."

"Just remember, with great power comes great responsibility."

"Well played." Her smile held a hint of mischief. "For that I say we skip the tabbouleh and go for pizza."

She felt the color drain from her face as memories of Blake washed over her. Thoughts of his death and her own guilt battered her moments before the familiar wave of nausea hit. "I can't eat pizza. I'm sorry."

Her expression turned sympathetic. "Bad experience?"

"The worst."

"I have so much to learn about you." She touched her cheek gently, her voice a whisper. "You know, I've heard there's a great Mediterranean place close by. We should check it out."

Eliot questioned the necessity of her task the entire time she sat at the table filling little rectangles with information that could already be found on the papers she consulted. She guessed these weren't the only records of donations pledged and received. But Harper insisted she needed the information in one easy-to-access location. It sounded like busywork to her, but it was busywork that gave her an excuse to spend more time in her company. And for that she was willing to pay the price of learning everything she'd avoided knowing about spreadsheets.

She would have liked to spend time with her that didn't involve a series of menial (and possibly unnecessary) tasks in the name of humanitarianism. It would be nice to have a conversation that wasn't subject to a dozen interruptions and peppered with oddly endearing micromanagement and friendly reminders to do the things she'd been successfully accomplishing since the second day of this partnership.

Not that they hadn't talked. They'd managed to squeeze some meaningful content into their staccato exchanges. That's how she'd been treated to the chronicle of Emilia's steadfast friendship and learned of the unfathomable loss of Harper's father just a few months after her brother's death. As usual, she avoided discussing the specifics of that first tragic loss, or anything related to her brother. Maybe she always would keep that part of her past hidden, but Eliot hoped not. She wanted to be trusted, a confidant. It would just take time and apparently a superabundance of volunteer hours coupled with mastery of spreadsheets.

"Here's a question." Eliot paused her attack on the dwindling to-be-entered pile and looked into her warm brown eyes, her breath catching (imperceptibly, she hoped). "The fundraiser is in just over a week. Shouldn't you have more help?"

"Are you suggesting you aren't enough?" Harper's playful smile knocked her even further off kilter.

"Or that this alleged fundraiser of yours is just an elaborate ruse to spend time with me."

"I guess you'll find out next weekend."

Their dinner arrived then, interrupting their conversation once more. Though her growling stomach pleaded with her to stop working, she was so close to finishing. One lone slip of paper stood between her and the satisfaction of a job well done. And, more importantly, time to focus non-surreptitiously on Harper. Even though she would keep working on whatever task caused her to frown adorably and run her fingers absently through her hair, Eliot would feel infinitely less guilt watching her do so if she had completed at least one task.

So, ignoring her hunger and the resounding crunch of Harper enjoying a baba ganoush laden carrot, she filled in the proper rectangles with the donor information and pledged amount, just as she'd done innumerable times before. But when she went to add the corresponding donation data, it wasn't there. It wasn't anywhere. She reread her notes and the instructions she thought she no longer needed, double checked her work and still came up short.

"Did you assign this task to any of your other volunteers? Assuming they exist."

"And decrease your torment? I wouldn't dream of it."

"So, they wouldn't have information on a donation that seems to be missing?"

"How big a donation?" She took another noisy bite, apparently unfazed by this development. Maybe missing donations were common in the world of non-profits, or maybe she was expecting an inconsequential figure.

"Ten thousand dollars."

Her chewing stopped abruptly, and she grabbed both the laptop and the page that Eliot had been puzzling over. She nodded gently as she read, almost like she was nudging the information into place. That, or she was having some kind of fit that Eliot was wildly unqualified to handle.

"This is one of our new corporate donors. The man I spoke with was kind of preoccupied when he made the pledge. He may have forgotten."

"Do people generally flake on five-figure donations?"

"This is easily fixed. They probably just need a reminder. I'll take care of it tomorrow." She closed the file and returned to her dinner.

"That's it? You'll just politely remind them to fork over ten grand in the morning?"

"I could do it now, but I think they've probably gone home for the day."

"You're not at all concerned about this?"

"I'm concerned. That's a big hit for us to take, especially with the event being so close. But what can I do right now?"

"Pass the hummus?" she suggested, bewildered that someone who could so calmly face such a sizable loss could be equally undone by the thought of pizza.

"Isn't there anything you can do?" Harper's entire body trembled, and her chest constricted, but somehow she managed not to crumble as she listened to the sweetly sympathetic woman tell her that her donation wasn't coming. "Can I talk to Josh? He promised this money two months ago. We were counting on it."

"Josh doesn't even work here anymore."

"Isn't there anyone I can speak to? Someone who can help us out?" She heard her voice break and didn't care. Maybe the sound of her desperation would pry open the purse strings of this woman who was probably very nice under other circumstances.

"I wish there were, but it's the end of the fiscal year, and we've already spent all of our charity budget. I'm awfully sorry about this."

"Maybe next year," she said, doubting there would be a next year for her carnival. The treasurer, Phoebe, had expressed concerns about it from the beginning, but Harper had promised it would be not just a success but a triumph. Now she would be remembered for losing a ten-thousand-dollar donation and a moderately successful event that likely didn't need to be replicated.

"Well, I just feel terrible about this," the woman said, and she did sound upset. "I know it's not the same, but I can give you fifty dollars, if that would help."

"That's very kind. Thank you," she said and walked the woman through the online donation process. "Only nine thousand nine hundred and fifty dollars to go," she groaned as she walked out the door.

CHAPTER TWENTY-FOUR

Harper walked blindly, not realizing until she saw the lake that she had headed east. The near perfection of the day, with its beatifically blue sky and the cool, gentle breeze off the lake that alleviated the heat of the midday sun, was lost on her but not on the teeming hordes of people clamoring to enjoy time outside. Fortunately for her they were too busy basking in the sunshine (or posting about it on social media) to notice the crying young woman in their midst.

She needed to tell someone about this disaster, and without hesitating, she called Eliot. She probably should let Phoebe and the rest of the board know, but she still had the delusional belief that she could somehow fix this. Besides, she wanted to feel better, not worse.

"Are you okay? Tell me what happened?" Just the sound of Eliot's voice, and the sympathy it held soothed her. But she'd need more than comforting words and a soft, familiar voice. She needed money.

Between shuddering breaths (the aftermath of her tearful reaction to the bad news), she explained the story of her missing donation, ending with the sweet (if wildly insufficient) donation from the woman who had delivered the worst news she'd received since her freshman year of high school.

"You can have everything in my savings account. That won't cover even half of what you need, but it's yours."

"I can't take your savings, Eliot."

"Of course you can. You need donations and I'm donating."

"That's too much to ask."

"You didn't ask, and I want to help you. You don't need to do this alone."

"I'm not alone. Just knowing that makes me think I can take care of this without depleting your savings."

"Then at least let me help you tonight."

"I'd love that. Thank you."

She felt somehow lighter and more grounded after talking to Eliot. She still had no idea how to pull ten thousand dollars out of thin air, but the urge to keep walking until the lake swept her away from her problems was beginning to subside. Until she turned around to see Caroline smiling at her.

"What are you doing here?"

"Taking a walk, same as you."

"Have you been following me?" She suddenly felt vulnerable in ways she'd never imagined.

"I saw you walk past when I was heading out for lunch, and I decided to catch up with you."

"Why?"

"So we can talk."

"We have nothing to talk about. You're married. I'm not interested in being your side piece. Our business is officially concluded. But do give my best to the missus." She turned to walk away—run if necessary—but Caroline grabbed her arm.

"I need to talk to you. I need to apologize, to do whatever you want to make this right. I miss you. I want you back."

"There isn't an apology in the universe that's compelling enough to make up for what you did." She pulled herself free from her grasp. "And there is absolutely nothing that you can do to get me back. What is it going to take to make you understand that?"

"I don't believe you. There has to be something I can do. I love you." Her voice took on a pleading tone, and she latched onto her upper arms. "Please don't shut me out."

"I can't do this right now." She pushed her away and stepped back, out of her reach. She wanted to scream at her, to unleash her rage. "You are so unbelievably selfish. I just—" She took a deep breath and collected herself as much as possible. "My fundraiser is a week from tomorrow, and I just lost a major donor, so now I have to somehow come up with ten thousand dollars, so I'm sorry, but I don't have time to argue with you about our nonexistent future together. You're just going to have to figure that out on your own."

She turned and walked away without another word, fueled by anger but feeling an intoxicating sense of satisfaction.

"You don't happen to have ten thousand dollars you can spare, do you?" It wasn't the best way to start a phone call, but Eliot didn't have time for pleasantries.

"I have a child with a major medical crisis being treated in the American healthcare system and another kid on the way. How much extra cash do you think I have?" Georgie replied.

"Apparently not ten k." She slumped on her couch, feeling like a shit for asking her sister for money. Scott, apparently concurring with that unsavory opinion, hopped off the couch and without so much as a glance back at her, sauntered off toward the bedroom.

"What is this about?" To her credit, Georgie sounded at least as intrigued as she did annoyed.

"Harper lost a big donor. The fundraiser will be okay without that money, but it won't be the success it should be. She's panicked about it, and—" She sighed and dropped her head into her hands. "I'm just trying to help."

"Have you considered asking Mom?"

"Absolutely not."

"You've been getting along lately. Mostly. You should cash in while it lasts."

"Because that's the best way to cultivate lasting peace between us. I couldn't ask her."

"But you can ask me?"

"You're not an inch from retirement. And she doesn't have that kind of money to throw around, but even if she did, it should be for her granddaughter. She is experiencing a major medical crisis, you know."

"I'm sorry I can't help you and your friend. Is she still a friend? Where do we stand on that?"

"It's still unclear." She sighed again, wondering what she could do to help.

Why didn't she have rich friends? Not one of the people she was close enough to ask a giant favor of was poised to shell out the kind of money Harper needed. She even considered asking her biological father for help, but their last lengthy conversation had been about her change of address a year and a half ago. He wasn't likely to become the benefactor of a cause he'd never heard of for a woman who might never be as significant to his largely estranged daughter as she would like.

The situation was a disaster, but not a complete one, she thought as she looked at the balance in her savings account. It had taken her a while to get her balance that high, but she could do it again, especially with the trajectory her career was on. But even if it took until she was ninety, what did it matter? It was just money, not nearly as important as the person it could help in this moment.

She grabbed her keys, ready to head to the bank for a cashier's check in the amount of her paltry savings, when her doorman called to announce a visitor.

Harper ran into work breathless and apologetic. Given her donation disappointment plus the surprise encounter with her ex, she was fifteen minutes late, and poor Meri, who got stuck covering the reception desk in her absence, had been trapped talking to Doug for far too long. She had no way of knowing how long the conversation had lasted, of course, but any amount of time talking to Doug was far too long, particularly if you were female.

"Nice of you to join us, sweetheart. We were just starting to wonder if you got lost."

"I just got held up." She plastered her fake smile on, resisting the urge to point out that she'd successfully made it to work almost every day for the past ten months. Barring brain death, she could find her way there in her sleep. "I'm sorry, Meri. I'll make it up to you."

"It's ok—"

"Are you going to make it up to the rest of us?" He leered at her, inspiring a wave of nausea.

"Excuse me?"

"Meri here wasn't the only one put out by your absence. She has her own work to do. Those emails aren't going to type themselves."

"I think the emails will be fine, but if she needs help, I also know how to type."

"That's a generous offer, honey, but to be perfectly honest, there's a reason we want you sitting behind this desk greeting people, and it's not your typing skills."

"You are a complete ass." The words fell out of her mouth before she realized they were forming, but she wasn't sorry. She was getting good at standing up for herself, and the surprised look on his face—like he finally realized she had a functioning brain—was worth it. "Have you realized that every woman in this office avoids you? We would rather take forty flights of stairs than get in an elevator with you. It's like you were transported here from the fifties and your brain can't handle the fact that us womenfolk aren't here for your amusement. You need industrial strength sexual harassment training. And you're boring. I quit." She looked to Meri, ready to apologize to the poor woman who would be stuck at this desk for the foreseeable future. Instead she was met with a massive, appreciative grin.

"Sweetheart, you don't mean that. Let's go to my office and talk."

"I don't want to talk to you in a crowded stadium. I'm certainly not going to go to your office." She grabbed the few possessions she had there and headed for the elevators. "And for the record, my name is Harper, not sweetheart."

With that, she walked out the door feeling elated and wanting to share this moment with the one person she knew would be proud of her.

CHAPTER TWENTY-FIVE

"Hi." Harper stood there in Eliot's doorway looking shyly determined, her pristine business attire an odd counterpoint to the wild look in her eye. "Can I come in?" She didn't wait for an answer.

"Not that I'm not happy to see you, but what are you doing here?"

"I wanted to see you." She strode into the living room, narrowly avoiding an entanglement with Scott, who believed he was the inspiration for every visitor.

"What's on your mind?"

"It's been a strange day. I quit my job and I confronted Caroline. I've basically been brutally honest with everyone I've encountered in the last hour or so. I've been a big hit with the jackass set today. But I realized I wasn't being honest with myself. Or you. And I need to be. I need to—this is too hard to say."

Eliot's mind was still on the Caroline part of Harper's little speech. What was Caroline doing back in the picture? Why were they talking? Shouldn't she be long gone? But then Harper's lips touched hers, the mental chatter stopped, and Eliot zeroed in on the incredible feeling of amazingly soft lips and an insistent tongue. Strong hands moved to her waist, pulling her closer, and if not for the strength of the arms now holding her, she wasn't sure she could have supported her own weight with her currently useless knees.

"You were saying something?" she gasped when their kiss broke. They stood encircled in one another's arms, their foreheads touching, her body trembling.

"Was I?"

"Maybe if you re-create the moment, you'll remember."

Their lips met again, hungrily, without restraint, and as their kiss deepened, her hands explored Harper, who, it seemed, would never cease to surprise her. Gently, Eliot caressed her face, savoring the soft skin beneath her fingers as they drifted from cheek to jaw and down her throat. When she heard Harper groan and felt the vibration in her fingertips, tenderness gave way to carnal need. She pulled her closer with one hand on the small of her back while the other hand moved to her full breasts, caressing them both before pinching an erect nipple. Her hips rocked involuntarily at the soft moan she elicited.

Meanwhile, Harper's hands roamed freely. Eliot felt her strong, sure fingers everywhere, grazing her breasts, stroking her back and then dropping to cup her ass. With each touch she stirred an already potent desire. Harper tugged at Eliot's shirt, breaking their kiss only long enough to pull it over her head, leaving a trail of goosebumps across her bare skin. Overwhelmed with sensation, Eliot steered them clumsily toward the bedroom, dimly aware that, for once, Scott didn't make a tripping hazard of himself.

By the time they reached the bed, they were both topless and breathing hard. She'd managed to unzip Harper's skirt, which fell to the floor moments before she fell back onto the bed, Eliot tumbling on top of her. Eliot's mouth immediately latched onto a breast, savoring the contrast of soft flesh surrounding rock hard nipple. She could linger there for an eternity, but there were more urgent matters. She lifted her head, looking into Harper's eyes. "Is this all right?"

For an answer, Harper pulled her in for another crushing kiss before unbuttoning her jeans. She dipped her hand inside, groaning at the evidence of Eliot's need. Her hips jerked in response, and she felt Harper smile into their kiss. Resisting the almost overwhelming urge to be taken, Eliot shifted out of her reach, instantly feeling more than just the physical loss. Slowly, almost reverently, she slid Harper's panties off. Just as deliberately, she traced the smooth, strong muscles of Harper's calves and thighs, savoring the journey back toward her need. Harper's breathing grew shallow and her body trembled with her desire until Eliot reached her center and she gasped, her hips moving faster in her urgency. Eliot increased the pressure of her touch until Harper cried out, pulling her close and rocking against her.

Harper hadn't stopped moving before she reached for Eliot again, pulling off her pants and zeroing in on her need. Eliot couldn't help the guttural moan that tore from her throat as Harper entered her. She ground herself against her, reveling in the sensation at the same time as she wanted to lose all control. She held off until Harper took her breast into her mouth, her tongue circling Eliot's nipple, bringing her to the edge of orgasm and then crashing over on wave after wave of sensation.

Harper woke to find Scott staring at her, his expression clearly judgmental. He blinked at her once, and then deeming her not only insufficient to satisfy his needs but also an impediment to that satisfaction, he strode away, his tail flicking with obvious irritation.

They'd fallen asleep in each other's arms, and even now, a tattooed arm lay across Harper's midsection, holding her close. She turned to look at Eliot, the soft light of the late afternoon filtering in through the blinds. When she stretched and rolled onto her back, Harper took advantage of the opportunity.

Straddling her hips, she began tracing the intricate lines of her many tattoos. She'd admired them from a distance, and more than once as they'd worked together, she'd studied them surreptitiously, trying to discern the various designs and whether there was any sort of pattern or logic behind the artwork that adorned her arms. Now was Harper's chance for a full-on examination.

"Is there something you're looking for?" She stretched again and squirmed beneath her when her knuckles grazed the side of her breast.

"Other women's names." She continued her search, running her fingers delicately along the outlines of birds, flowers, even a mermaid, finding nothing incriminating.

"If you're worried about other women, you don't need to be."

"Please. I've seen you with other women. You flirt as naturally as you breathe."

"But that doesn't mean anything. It's just conversation, and not with anyone I had a long-term relationship with. You, on the other hand . . ."

"What do you mean?"

"You said you talked to Caroline today?"

At the mention of her ex's name, Harper stopped her search and looked her in the eye, startled by the insecurity she saw there. "I also told you I quit my job."

"But I'm not worried about that."

"I am. I'm unemployed."

"You still have the bakery and an in with the owner. She'll probably let you work more hours in the few days it takes you to find a new job, one that you don't hate and that's deserving of your talents. I don't know what happened, but I do know that the problem was them, not you. You'll be fine because you're too smart and determined and passionate not to be."

She blushed at the praise until she reflected on the first part of the conversation. "You're worried about Caroline?"

"She hasn't been your ex very long, and it's a bit late now, but—" She swallowed hard and looked away. "I can't be your rebound."

"That's not why I came here. That's not what I want."

"I couldn't take it."

Eliot sounded almost desperate. Whether because she hadn't heard or didn't believe her didn't matter. Harper touched her cheek gently, drawing her attention. "I don't want her. I ran away from her today, and I came to you." She kissed her gently, hoping to offer some kind of reassurance. "I chose you." They kissed once more, tenderly, and Eliot held her close. "But that doesn't mean I'm going to end my search."

"Fine." She threw her arms wide, but Harper hesitated.

"Do you really think I'll be okay?"

"I know it." They kissed for a while longer, reigniting their desire. "But first you have a fundraiser to finish planning. It's coming up fast. We should probably get to work."

"It can wait a little bit longer."

CHAPTER TWENTY-SIX

The next week passed in a blur. Even without the drudgery of a nine-to-five job occupying a good portion of her days, Harper still found herself scrambling to get everything done. By the time she called it a day, she was exhausted and overwhelmed by her never-ending to-do list. Whenever possible, she spent the night with Eliot, finding surprising pleasure in the simple act of sleeping in her arms all night (or as much of the night as they actually slept). Cuddling was officially her second favorite thing to do with Eliot.

But on the nights when Eliot tended bar or spent time with her niece, once again home from the hospital, Harper worked on the event until it become impolite to others around her to do so. She spent as much time as she could at the venue, supervising the event set up and putting out the million fires that seemed to flare up simultaneously, threatening both her composure and the fundraiser's success. She met with volunteers and vendors, and in her brief and infrequent snippets of down time, she worked on reversing that ten-thousand-dollar deficit that jeopardized her event. Even after exhausting every avenue she could imagine, she still came up far too short.

Aside from their short meeting to discuss Em's booth at the carnival, she'd seen her only briefly, during her regularly scheduled shift at the bakery the morning after she quit her job and slept with Eliot. She still couldn't believe how well Em took the news that she was more or less unemployed.

"Business is good, right?"

"People love cake," was her non-committal response as she deposited evidence of that love in the ever-growing pile of dirty dishes beside her.

"Enough that you need more help?"

"Who do you know that's looking for a job?"

"Funny story," she said before sharing the details of her life's recent upheaval, starting with Caroline's ambush and ending with a vague account of where and how she'd spent the last half of her day. "Are you mad?"

"Only that you didn't tell me sooner about Eliot."

"I've been here ten minutes. How much sooner could I have told you?"

"I've been pushing for this for weeks. You should have called me the minute it happened."

"I was a little busy."

"Obviously, you could have waited until you finished."

"I just told you that unless you start paying me more, I won't make my half of rent, which really means you're going to pay our full rent, no matter what, but you're upset because I waited a few hours to update you on my relationship status?"

"There are more important things than rent."

"Like paying my student loans?"

"Like standing up for yourself and getting out of that job. I'm proud of you for finally confronting Doug, although I doubt he heard what you were saying over his internal soundtrack of 'Nasty feminist bitch' playing on a constant loop."

"Still felt good to say it." She reflected on the supreme satisfaction of her Doug tirade. Even if she had to wash Em's dishes for eternity, it was worth it. And since she hadn't imperiled a decade-long friendship by her rash decision-making, it seemed that, in spite of going wildly off track, her life was more or less working out.

"Now," she poured them each a fresh cup of coffee and rested against the counter behind her, "tell me all about Eliot."

And that had been the extent of it. Throughout the morning, Em had insisted on hearing as many details as could be crammed into the spurts of time they had before their responsibilities called them elsewhere. It was an odd but welcome experience to have a relationship that her best friend supported.

Not everything had gone so smoothly, however. She'd received three texts from Caroline in as many days, all of them apologetic and pleading, and not one of them indicating that her "Ignore her and maybe she'll go away" strategy was having any effect. Harper considered changing her number, but with the fundraiser so close, it would be a logistical nightmare to update her contact information with the scores of people who needed to reach her. So she braced herself for the next willfully oblivious communication and counted down the days until she could cut one more tie to her unfortunate past.

She also hadn't gotten the support from her mother that she'd hoped for. She didn't expect her to celebrate her startling new employment status, but she also hadn't anticipated being quite the letdown that she apparently was. While her mother never went so far as to chastise her, her disappointment was clear.

"But honey, you don't have another job lined up. How are you going to get by?"

"I've already talked to Em about expanding my role at the bakery."

"What about the long-term? You don't want to work at the bakery for the rest of your life, do you?" The tone in her voice walked a fine line between reactionary judgment and maternal concern, and Harper tried to focus on the latter.

"If it means I don't have to subject myself to the leering advances of a world-class misogynist, then I'll gladly help my best friend with her business."

"I know you weren't happy there and I know why. Even if I don't sound it, I'm glad you won't have to deal with that man anymore. I just wish you hadn't jeopardized your own well-being in the process. Are you at least looking for more work?"

"Once the fundraiser is behind me, my priority will be to find a new job."

Her mother sighed as if she wanted to push for more urgency, but after a painful moment of uncertain near silence, she relented and asked about the carnival.

And so, with her mother's concerned interest, her best friend's blessing and genuine support from the woman she wasn't sure if she could call her girlfriend, she tackled the final day of preparations. A thousand last-minute details needed her attention, not the least of which was the donation that slipped away. All that sustained her were thoughts of seeing Eliot that night after she got off work and the impending relief of her event's (hopefully triumphant) completion.

"You left your bra on the coffee table." Alice dangled the aforementioned article of clothing between her fingers. She'd stopped by unannounced and didn't seem eager to make it a quick visit. "This isn't yours, is it?"

"No comment." Eliot tried to snatch it from her but didn't move quickly enough. Instead of playing keep-away, she merely glared and folded her arms.

"I'm going to get it out of you eventually. You should just tell me now."

"Or I could respect her privacy."

"How about if I guess and you tell me if I'm wrong."

She frowned but said nothing as her friend studied the evidence.

"I think this specimen," she held the silky pink number up for examination, "might belong to a certain young woman with strong philanthropic tendencies."

"Wow. It's almost like you're a detective."

"And a damn good one."

"Too bad your friend credentials are a bit shaky right now."

"After all I did to unite the two of you? You'd think I could at least get a 'Thank you.'"

"Thank you. Now why are you here?" She managed to retrieve Harper's bra before continuing on her path to her drawing studio to pack up her supplies for the morning. She didn't need more than an hour to set up at the venue, but she planned to be there with Harper from start to finish, helping her with whatever she needed. Since she had to work that night, she intended to be packed up and ready to go so that when the adorably predictable (not to mention unnecessary) reminder about the big day tomorrow came, she could ease Harper's stress and panic ever so slightly with evidence of her preparedness.

"You're in a foul mood for someone whose home decor prominently features another woman's undergarments. What's wrong? Is it Audrey?"

"Audrey has been doing great."

She'd returned home from the hospital four days earlier, and so far remained healthy, or as healthy as a seven-year-old fighting cancer could be considered. "She's sad she can't come to the carnival tomorrow, but we can't risk bringing her and her compromised immune system into such a big crowd. Harper has been trying to figure out how to bring the carnival to her, but for now all we've come up with is the promise of lots of cotton candy and maybe a balloon animal."

"Sounds like things are going well with Harper, so again I ask, what's with the teen-in-a-snit impersonation?"

"What if things stop going well with Harper?" She double-checked the contents of her marker case, carefully keeping her back to her friend.

"What has you convinced so early on that's it's going to fail?"

"I'm not convinced. Just concerned." She braced herself for the look of pity she was about to inspire. "About the ex-girlfriend."

"What about her? Is she still in the picture?"

"I don't think so. Harper says no but I'm still worried."

"Do you have reason to believe she would lie to you?"

She shook her head, feeling more ridiculous by the second.

"Then maybe you should trust her. Focus on you and her and let her past stay in the past."

"You're right. I'm being an idiot."

"Thanks for not making me say it."

Late that night, she got home from work to find Harper sound asleep on her couch, Scott curled in the crook of her arm, purring noisily. Her lips were slightly parted, and a lock of her hair had come loose from her ponytail and fallen across her forehead. Eliot wanted to draw this moment, to capture the innocent beauty tucked away in her living room. But they had a big day, starting in a few short hours, and they both needed rest. She knelt beside the couch, and after evicting a grumbling Scott, gently kissed her forehead.

"I missed you." Harper pulled her in for a proper kiss that threatened the likelihood of sleep. "I'm glad you're home."

"Are you ready for tomorrow?" She nodded and yawned expansively. "Looks like you need to get some more sleep."

"That's not all I need." She leaned in for another kiss.

"Well, that's all you're getting tonight."

They kissed once more, a lingering, stimulating kiss that ended with Harper biting her lower lip. "We'll see about that."

CHAPTER TWENTY-SEVEN

If Harper had a weather catalogue, she couldn't have specially ordered a more perfect day for her event. As she strode through the space in the last moments before they opened to the public, the sun peeked out from behind one of the few fluffy white clouds dotting the bright blue sky. The temperature hovered in the mid-seventies, and her volunteers and vendors all seemed happy and ready to go. Even Phoebe, the skeptical treasurer, seemed impressed by the event, though she was apparently comfortable withholding any outright praise until the final numbers told her just how impressed she should be. With so much going right, Harper couldn't shake the ominous feeling of an impending catastrophe.

But as attendance gradually increased—with people playing games, sampling the carnival fare and obviously enjoying themselves—her fear began to subside. She made regular sweeps of the makeshift fairgrounds, and each time she completed the circuit, she came to the same conclusion: all of her hard work was paying off. A few problems cropped up here and there— one of the credit card machines at the entrance went down for twenty minutes and the head balloon animal clown had a splint on his finger, seriously impacting his productivity. Nothing that couldn't be dealt with, but it was just enough to prevent her from relaxing entirely. Or from spending any length of time lurking near the caricature booth.

She passed by a few times as Eliot chatted amicably with the person perched in the chair in front of her. Each time Eliot winked before turning her easy charm back on her model, and each time Harper's stomach dipped and she forgot what she was supposed to be doing. She was tempted to wait in line for her own drawing, but even if she had the time to spare, she doubted the wisdom of exposing herself to the intimacy of her gaze in public.

"How are the donations coming along?" She'd just passed Eliot again (and recovered from the subsequent swoon) and was approaching the ring toss when Phoebe flagged her down, the musical tinkle of plastic colliding with glass a pleasant counterpoint to her wheedling voice.

"At least as well as when you asked me fifteen minutes ago." The smell of fresh popcorn reached her, reminding her that she'd skipped breakfast. And dinner the night before. Come to think of it, she actually wasn't sure when she last ate.

"I'm just concerned that, as much fun as everyone seems to be having, we're not pulling in the dollars we should be."

"That's what you said earlier, but—" She heard someone call her name and turned to find Caroline heading straight for her.

Every part of her wanted to run, except her feet apparently, as they refused to move. She just stood there, frozen to the earth, mouth agape, as Phoebe droned on about donations and a blithely smiling Caroline bore down on her. Worse, Eliot sat at the other end of the aisle, watching as this nightmare unfolded, her expression growing darker with each step Harper's ex took. Harper's misery intensified when Caroline bounded up and greeted her with an unwelcome kiss.

She immediately pushed her away and looked to Eliot, just in time to catch her glower before she walked away. Her heart sank, and when she saw Caroline still in front of her, grinning as if she hadn't just sauntered in and ruined everything, the potential impact on her position with Allies was the only thing keeping her anger in check.

"What are you doing here?" she hissed.

"It's the big day. I wanted to be part of your victory."

"Well, that remains to be seen," Phoebe chimed in, her skepticism still firmly in place.

"I have something for you."

"I'm not interested in anything you have to offer." She tried to walk away, but the crowd pressed around her, preventing a retreat.

"Not even this?" With a flourish, she presented a check for ten thousand dollars, holding the small slip of paper up for her examination. Behind her, Phoebe stopped muttering about Harper's potential failure long enough to gasp. Harper ground her teeth in frustration at the same time as a wave of unwelcome gratitude washed over her.

"Why can't you just leave me alone?"

"Is that any way to treat a donor?" Caroline grinned again, confident that she'd claimed some victory.

And in a way she had. No matter her personal feelings about Caroline, Harper couldn't refuse her donation. So far today she'd been nickel-and-diming her way into the black, but as the practically drooling Phoebe would be sure to point out, this money was vital for Allies. So despite the overwhelming urge to join the witness protection program just to escape Caroline, she instead had to accept this connection, and she had to do it with a smile.

"Thank you." She immediately passed the check to Phoebe in the vain hope that it would send her scurrying toward her ledger, but rather than repelling her, it acted more like super glue.

"Yes, thank you." Phoebe shook her hand aggressively, and Caroline, obviously uncomfortable with her enthusiastic fawning, looked to Harper for help. "Such a generous donation deserves a little more enthusiasm than that, don't you think, Harper?" Phoebe elbowed her painfully in the ribs. "Maybe you can give our donor a tour. Show her behind the scenes. Wouldn't that be fun?"

In that moment Harper could think of nothing that sounded less fun. "I'm afraid I'm needed elsewhere."

Phoebe sidled even closer and whispered, "This is an amazing opportunity for you to cultivate a relationship with a substantial donor. Maybe connect with more supporters like her. You could really prove your worth to the organization."

"I can't," she spoke through clenched teeth.

"Think of what it would mean for Allies." She whispered, as if the subject of their hushed discussion was somehow unaware that she inspired their far from stealthy conversation.

"I have and I'm telling you that I can't do this. Please don't ask me to."

"I'm going to have to insist. Consider what a donation like that deserves."

She could explain her reservations. They'd known each other for years, and though they'd never developed a friendship, she'd considered their relationship collegial. But the eyes that met hers were so full of dollar signs there was no room for compassion.

"You're absolutely right." Fake smile in place, she faced her ex. "Thank you for that unexpected donation. Such generosity deserves more than a volunteer who's still proving her worth. You deserve full access not just to the event, but also to our treasurer, Phoebe, who wants to give you a private tour." She allowed herself a moment to savor the horrified look on Caroline's face as her plan backfired. Phoebe, on the other hand, seemed delighted at the opportunity to monopolize their newest patron. "If you'll excuse me, I need to go tend to an urgent matter."

Without another word, she pushed herself through the crowd, determined to talk to Eliot.

It didn't take more than half a second of watching Harper kiss her ex to make Eliot abandon her booth. Fueled by misery, anger and more than a little embarrassment, she excused herself in the middle of a drawing and fled the scene. She didn't care where she went as long as it didn't include the panoramic view of Harper kissing another woman. She wound her way through the crowd loitering near the cotton candy vendor and forced herself past the varying displays of athletic prowess from those testing their strength at the Strongman Game, the occasional clang of a bell ringing out the proof of some participant's virility. But she didn't get much farther before her conscience overrode her emotions. Overwhelmed with guilt, she stopped abruptly, causing a minor human traffic jam beside the soft pretzel stand.

No matter what she was going through, that didn't diminish the importance of the cause she'd signed on to help. She'd made a commitment, and just because she'd made it to a woman who didn't seem to understand the meaning of the word, that didn't mean she had to abandon her own integrity. She would finish the work she'd promised to do because (unlike some people) she understood the importance of behaving honorably. Nor did her own suffering negate the significance of this event to Clara, the little girl who had looked crestfallen at Eliot's premature departure.

Prior to Harper's betrayal, Clara had been bouncing in her seat and chattering excitedly about her favorite superheroes, an impressive array that included Captain Marvel, Kitty Pryde and Eliot's own favorite, Kate Bishop. She'd been hesitant at first about having her portrait drawn (understandably so). What ten-year-old harbored a desire for a stranger's rendering of herself? But she'd submitted to her mother's urging, and once she learned that Eliot was "a real live comic book artist," she grew increasingly animated. And then Eliot had run off without any explanation. Now, as the crowd maneuvered around her, jostling her in their eagerness to reach the next shiny attraction, the thought that she'd disappointed Clara or, worse, dimmed her enthusiasm for comic books in any way crushed Eliot, so not wanting to hurt anyone like she had just been hurt, she returned to her booth.

"I'm sorry, Clara. I felt a little sick," she apologized to the little girl whose earlier enthusiasm was now tainted with uncertainty.

"Are you all right?"

"I will be if you let me finish your drawing."

Clara beamed at her, and they picked up where they had left off.

Not unlike Eliot at that age, Clara asked three thousand questions, barely pausing long enough for an answer to any of them. She inquired what books Eliot had worked on, who was her favorite character, was that different from her favorite character to draw, had she ever met anyone cool like Sana Takeda or Jill Thompson or Kelly Sue DeConnick? Eliot answered every question not only because it distracted her from periodically berating herself for ever being so stupidly optimistic about Harper being over her ex, but also because she had been that little girl, finding solace in the pages of her favorite comics and community among those like her, who craved the next book in a series. Her intense desire to be elsewhere had nothing to do with the budding comic book geek before her, and she refused to be a contributing factor to anything other than a substantial and long-abiding fondness for the world of comics.

So, she stayed. She drew and discussed the minutia of comic book history, and when Harper rushed up to her wanting to talk, she tersely declined, pointing to the almost complete portrait of her young patron and citing her need to focus as valid reasons that she couldn't be disturbed.

"How about when you finish with this?"

"I need to keep working." She ignored the pleading tone in Harper's voice.

"You don't have a line right now, and I think you need a break. Don't you?"

"I think if you had any idea what I need, you wouldn't have made out with your, I'm guessing, former ex where I could witness it."

"I know what it looked like, but that's not what happened. That's why I want to talk."

"I'm busy." She pointed again to her drawing. "But if you really want to talk to someone, I'm sure Caroline would be happy to hear whatever you have to say." With that she turned her back on her and focused all her attention on Clara and her portrait.

Harper tried more than once to talk to Eliot, to no avail. Any time she neared her booth, either she was called away by some minor predicament, or she was ignored. For the interminable remainder of the day, the demands on her attention (as well as Eliot's complete disinterest in having that attention) made a meaningful conversation impossible. But it gave her time to think. When she wasn't resolving the million non-emergencies that demanded her attention or avoiding her ex, who refused to leave, even after Phoebe got her in her crosshairs, she considered her situation and what she could do about it.

No matter how she looked at the issue, the answer was always the same: the crux of her problem was Caroline. She'd broken up with her, wanted nothing to do with her, and in her mind, had made that clear. Nevertheless, she refused to leave. And as long as she stuck around, she would never have a shot at experiencing the kind of commitment her mother had talked about with Eliot. The more she contemplated what she could have with her—the connection, the flirting, the sex, the cuddling and all they had yet to discover together—the more she realized she wanted it.

But Caroline stood in her way, a big, blond roadblock to her freedom and happiness. Her obstinate refusal to let Harper go could ruin any chance she had with Eliot. It might have done that already, but she refused to accept that now. One problem at a time, and for now her problem was her lamentably resilient connection to her ex.

She had already quit her job and planned to change her phone number, cutting off potential access, but she realized she would have to do more. She confronted the very real possibility that she would have to move. Though she felt safer living with her excessively protective best friend in the building that her parents owned than she ever would living alone, she was far too easy to find at her current address.

Just as she was through Allies. If nothing else, Caroline had proven the extreme lengths she would go to keep Harper in her life, and there was no guarantee that she wouldn't do it again. Especially now that Phoebe had her sights on Caroline and her potential battery of charity-minded associates, she might show up unannounced at any event and make Harper's life unbearable. She didn't want to limit her contributions (and by extension her potential advancement) any more than she wanted to dread her work.

As night fell and the event wound down, she realized what she needed. Moving against the tide of the departing crowd, she rushed to catch Eliot before she packed up and left, possibly for good.

"We need to talk." She grabbed her hand, refusing to take no for an answer.

CHAPTER TWENTY-EIGHT

Eliot stumbled through the event space as Harper dragged her along, dodging the volunteers and vendors who dismantled what they'd worked so hard to put together. Harper stopped abruptly once they'd reached the far back corner of the carnival. It wasn't exactly private, but it was as close as they were likely to get. And with the clamor and chaos of teardown surrounding them, it seemed like an oddly appropriate backdrop for their impending conversation.

"What are we doing?" She wrenched her hand free from Harper's grip. "It's been a long day and I just want to go home."

"That's what I want too."

She stepped closer, but Eliot dodged the hand that reached for hers. "Then say whatever is on your mind so we can put an end to this."

"I want to go home with you."

"Why? So you can kill time until she comes back? Thanks, but I'm not interested in being your distraction."

"I'm not interested in that either."

"Then what do you want?"

"If you listen to my mom, I want to hide from life. She thinks I settled for the kind of relationship I had with Caroline because I'm always trying to protect myself from getting hurt. What we had worked so well because she made it easy to stay detached while telling myself that our connection was real. But it wasn't. None of my relationships have been."

"I'm not sure why you're telling me this, unless your goal is to make me feel even worse about what I thought we had."

"I'm telling you because she was right. I kept myself closed off because it's too dangerous to commit to anyone. Loving someone meant pain, and that was too risky. Until now. You make me want to take that risk." Harper reached for her again, and though she didn't want to relinquish her anger so easily, she didn't retreat from her touch this time. She felt Harper's hand on her face, lifting her chin and forcing eye contact. "You make me want to take all kinds of risks. My life was so calm and predictable and boring before you walked into that restaurant and shook everything up. I quit my job and I ended my pretend relationship, and my plan for the future is terrifyingly vague. But no matter how turbulent and uncertain my life is, being with you—even just thinking of you—makes me feel less adrift. And I like that feeling. I want more of it. I want more of you."

Eliot wanted to believe her. But she couldn't pretend she hadn't witnessed the incredibly public display of affection that belied that statement just a few hours ago. "Then why were you kissing her?"

"I didn't want to kiss her. I didn't even want to see her. But she ambushed me, again. She's been doing that a lot lately."

"Which means she'll always be in your life, whether you want her there or not."

"It means I have to try harder to get away from her. It's one of the reasons I'm leaving Allies."

"You're what?" She couldn't quit. She was meant for this work, and she'd already given up so much.

"I'm quitting. This is my last event with them."

"You can't quit."

"As long as I'm connected to Allies, I'll be connected to her. Self-absorbed as she is, even she understands my dedication to this organization, so if she wants to find me, she'll come looking for me there."

"But you love Allies."

"I love the work, and I'm starting to see that Allies is only one way to do it. Because of you, I think maybe it's time for me to try something new."

Harper's eyes were brimming with hope and eagerness and a liberal dose of panic, and as she stared into the naked honesty of that expression, Eliot's reservations melted away. She'd gone from anger to heartbreak to hopeful joy, all in the span of about fifteen minutes. She offered a small smile and took her hand.

"So, tell me about this new thing you're going to try."

"I'm going to start my own charity, one like Allies but that also does all the things I wish they did." Instead of the backlash and doubt peddling that Harper braced for, Eliot whooped, drawing the attention of the people working around them. "You don't think it's a bad idea?"

"I think it's one of the best ideas I've ever heard. Peanut butter cups still top it, but this is a close second."

"High praise."

"What made you decide to do this?"

"You." It was difficult to tell in the dim light of the night sky and the rapidly dwindling carnival, but she swore Eliot—the most confident woman on the planet—blushed. "And lots of little things adding up. Do you know why I started volunteering with Allies?"

"Because your brother died."

"Because I let him die." At Eliot's aghast expression, Harper felt the familiar protective numbness creeping in, but she refused to disappear into it. "I was supposed to get him to come downstairs for dinner. He'd been sulking in his room for hours, but Mom wanted all of us to eat together. It wasn't a special meal or anything, just pizza from the Italian place down the street, but she insisted that we eat together as a family, and it was my job to make that happen. Only I was tired of him being in one of his moods. I didn't want to deal with him. I didn't want to beg him to be part of the family, so I avoided him until I couldn't help it. Once my dad showed up with the pizza, I couldn't put it off any longer. So I snuck a slice to sustain me for the long walk to his room. And that's when I found him."

"That wasn't your fault." Eliot pulled her into a tight embrace.

"I know that now. Most of the time. But it still felt like something I could have stopped if I hadn't been so stupid and selfish."

"You were a kid."

"And I don't ever want any other kid to go through that. I don't want any other little sisters to make that mistake because they don't know what to do or how to be supportive. I think I've done some good, but I know I can do more." Harper stepped back and looked into Eliot's eyes. "And I know that because of you. I look at you and all you do to nurture your dream, and I want that. I want to start my own organization. I want to risk everything and work harder than I've ever worked. And every night, I want to fall exhausted into your arms. Please say you want that too."

Eliot drew her close and with a soft, slow, lingering kiss, answered with the perfect yes.

EPILOGUE

"I think I'm in love." Harper gazed adoringly at the sleeping baby in her arms. She'd been holding him less than a minute when he opened his eyes for a moment before yawning and falling back to sleep. She wanted to hold him until his next birthday, but of all the people gathered to meet little Emmett, she had the least claim to him, as he was the only person in the room who was newer to the family than she was. Reluctantly, she handed him to his grandmother, earning a smile of thanks and praise.

"You look good holding a baby."

"Subtle, Ma," Eliot chastised gently, but as she sat with her niece in her lap and watched her hours-old nephew sleep through his welcome to the family, her grin conveyed a joy that not even her mother's campaign for more grandchildren could diminish.

"All I said was she looks good. I can't compliment your girlfriend now?"

"Since it's basically impossible not to, I'll allow it."

Harper knew she was blushing as she took the seat beside Eliot, rested her head on her shoulder and held her hand, their fingers linking immediately. She felt the same thrill as always when they touched, whether it was innocently holding hands or the more intimate touching that made her pulse race and her skin flushed just to consider. She shivered thinking of their connection, and Eliot planted a sweetly innocent kiss on her cheek. She actually felt her heart flutter and thought, not for the first time, that this was what her mother had been talking about. This moment and the million more like it she envisioned in their future was worth the remote and terrifying possibility of losing Eliot. She wouldn't trade it for anything.

"I love you," she whispered.

Eliot stared at her. "What did you just say?"

"I said I love you." She barely completed the sentence before Eliot kissed her, a kiss she could have easily lost herself in, not even caring that the entire DeSanto family was witness to this moment. If not for a pointed throat clearing somewhere behind her, she surely would have.

"And I love you." Eliot's words, her smile and her eyes, locked on Harper's and overflowing with love and longing, made Harper wonder how she'd ever thought she was better off living without this feeling.

"Quit being so grossly in love you two. One of us has been awake all night giving birth and has a low threshold for adorable that didn't come out of her." Georgie's smile belied her irritation. But just to secure her standing, she handed her the box Em had sent—a dozen blueberry and strawberry-frosted "baby" donuts.

"How's the new charity coming along?" Jimmy's cheeks were redder than usual, no doubt thanks to the vivid imagery his daughter had just introduced to the room. "Any luck so far?"

"It's slow going, but I'm making progress. And I did just secure my first full-fledged patron." She shared a lingering gaze with her as-yet biggest supporter. "Eliot is planning to donate all of her royalties from *Time the Avenger* to charity, and my little non-profit is one of her beneficiaries."

"It won't be that much." Eliot shrugged.

"I think it's going to be hugely successful, and I couldn't be prouder of what you've created."

"What *we* created." She hugged Audrey closer to her. "Which is why half of the royalties go toward Audrey's medical bills. Probably won't pay for much more than tissue, but—"

"Considering how much they charge for tissue, that's a generous offer." Carla offered a compliment for her eldest, something she'd been doing consistently lately. "Plus, I have it on good authority that you're one of the best. It's going to be a hit."

"Thank you." Eliot's genuine smile of gratitude lingered for a moment before she turned her attention back to Audrey, who was munching happily on a pink frosted donut. "I guess this means you need a sidekick now."

For an answer she yawned expansively. They'd let her stay up too late the night before, in part because Zizi was a sucker for her niece's doe eyes, but also because they were all too eager about meeting the new baby to sleep. Now, however, she seemed less than impressed.

"Aren't you excited to have a brother?" Harper asked.

"He doesn't really do much." She wrinkled her nose in his general direction.

"That will change," Georgie said and yawned to match her daughter.

"I'll tell you what I think then." She vacated her Zizi's lap and sat by her mother, who brushed a lock of her rapidly returning short, dark hair from her forehead. "Do you have a brother, Harper?"

"I used to."

"What happened to him?"

Eliot put a reassuring arm around her, and she savored the closeness, both physical and emotional. "He died."

"You can share my brother if you want."

"I'd like that very much."

Bella Books, Inc.

Women. Books. Even Better Together.

P.O. Box 10543
Tallahassee, FL 32302

Phone: 800-729-4992
www.bellabooks.com